H

Wolves of the Sundown Trail

WOLVES OF THE SUNDOWN TRAIL

A WESTERN TRIO

LES SAVAGE, JR.

FIVE STAR

An imprint of Thomson Gale, a part of The Thomson Corporation

THOMSON

™

GALE

Detroit • New York • San Francisco • New Haven, Conn. • Waterville, Maine • London

LIBRARY OF CONGRESS CATALOGING-IN-PUBLICATION DATA

Savage, Les.
  Wolves of the Sundown Trail : a western trio / by Les Savage.—1st ed.
    p. cm.—
  "A Five Star western" —T.p. verso.
  "Published in conjunction with Golden West Literary Agency" —T.p. verso.
    ISBN-13: 978-1-59414-510-0 (hardcover: alk. paper)
    ISBN-10: 1-59414-510-5 (hardcover: alk. paper)
    I. Title.
  PS3569.A826W65 2007
  813'.54—dc22   2007017456

First Edition. First Printing: October 2007.

Published in 2007 in conjunction with Golden West Literary Agency.

Printed in the United States of America on permanent paper
10 9 8 7 6 5 4 3 2 1

CONTENTS

★ ★ ★ ★ ★

THE LASH OF *SEÑORITA* SCORPION

★ ★ ★ ★ ★

Les Savage, Jr., narrated the adventures of Elgera Douglas, better known as *Señorita* Scorpion, in a series of seven short novels that originally appeared in *Action Stories,* published by Fiction House. She was, by far, the most popular literary series character to appear in this magazine in the nearly thirty years of its publication history. The fifth short novel in this series, "The Brand of Penasco," is included in *The Shadow in Renegade Basin: A Western Trio* (Five Star Westerns, 2000). The seventh, and last, story in the series, "The Sting of *Señorita* Scorpion," is collected in the eponymous *The Sting of Señorita Scorpion: A Western Trio* (Five Star Westerns, 2000). The short novel that began the series, "*Señorita* Scorpion," can be found in *The Devil's Corral: A Western Trio* (Five Star Westerns, 2003). This first story so pleased Malcolm Reiss, the general manager at Fiction House, that he wanted another story about her for the very next issue. The sequel, titled "The Brand of *Señorita* Scorpion," is collected in *The Beast in Cañada Diablo: A Western Trio* (Five Star Westerns, 2004). "Secret of the Santiago," third in the series, is collected in *Trail of the Silver Saddle* (Five Star Westerns, 2005). The fourth of the *Señorita* Scorpion stories was "The Curse of Montezuma," and is included in the eponymous book, *The Curse of Montezuma: A Western Trio* (Five Star Westerns, 2006). Savage's original title for the short novel that follows, and the last of the series to be collected, was "The Return of *Señorita* Scorpion." It was accepted by Fiction House in early March, 1947, and on March 11th the author was paid $500.00 for it, approximately 2 1/2¢ a word. The story was titled for publication "Lash of the Six-Gun Queen," and it was supposed to appear in the Fall, 1947 issue of *Action Stories*. In fact, the oil painting to be used on the cover for that issue had already been ordered from the graphic illustrator, Allen Anderson, and this painting did appear on the cover of the Fall, 1947 issue. What didn't appear in that issue was the new *Señorita* Scorpion story. It was published, instead, in the Winter, 1947 issue. In this continuation of the saga Les Savage, Jr., added a new character in the form of the first-person narrator, U.S. Marshal Powder Welles. At the time, Savage had begun experimenting with first-person narration in his Western stories. While there was a certain novelty to these attempts by Savage, the author later abandoned this approach, and Welles never returns in later stories in the saga. Also by the time Savage came to write this short novel, he was making ample use of Ramon F. Adams's seminal *Western Words: A Dictionary of the Range, Cow Camp, and Trail*, first published in book form by the University of Oklahoma Press in 1944. These expressions, unfamiliar perhaps to some modern readers, are coin of the realm in that reference book. For its advent in book form here the text of this short novel has been restored, according to the author's original type-script.

I

Butcherknife Hill was about thirty miles north of the Mexican border, and they had told me in Alpine I would find him there. The first thing I thought, upon seeing him, was bull. That's exactly the way it bulged into my mind. Bull. And you don't know what that means really, unless you've seen a real, old-time mossyhorn sulking. Pure destruction with its tail switching. Shoulders so big and flanks so small he looks out of shape, almost awkward, till he moves. Cats don't have more grace. But he doesn't have to move. Just look in those little red eyes, and you've got it.

"Chisos Owens?" I said.

His eyes weren't red, though. They were the color of gunsmoke. He sat a big dun with an arched mane, and his Porter rig was double-girted the way all Texas men like them. His Levi's and old cotton shirt were so faded and soiled I couldn't tell the original color.

"Marshal Powder Welles?" he said. He had thin lips for such a heavy-boned face, and they barely moved over the words.

"News travels fast in the Big Bend," I said.

"We have a grapevine of sorts," he told me. "I heard you were in Alpine, inquiring after me. I don't know where the Scorpion is, Marshal, and, if I did, I wouldn't tell you."

My own Porter rig *creaked* as I leaned toward him. "That was a United States Senator the Scorpion murdered in Alpine, Owens. I work for the same government. Do I have to tell you the trouble you are going to get in for not helping me, or are we going somewhere and talk?"

The back of his hand was covered with pale blond hair, except where an old rope burn cut across it. He put his fingers around the saddle horn. There was a faint, distinct *popping* sound. It must have come from the cords on his wrist, standing out as big as dally ropes in that moment with the force of his grip. Then he lifted his shoulders in a shrug and led the way up to a line shack on the ridge. There was a cottonwood corral out back, and we turned our animals in there. A plank table and a pair of pegged-pine benches made up the furniture inside, with wall bunks at the rear and an old wood stove in one corner. He threw some chunks of mesquite on and filled the coffee pot from the water butt inside the door. I sat down at the table and took off my John B. to scratch my head.

"It's funny how the Mexicans tack on names like that," I said. "*Señorita* Scorpion. I understand it fits Elgera Douglas."

"It fits," he said.

"I understand you were in love with her."

He was turned away from me, when I said it, and bent over the stove. But his whole great frame seemed to lift a little with the breath he took. Finally he turned around and lowered himself to the bench opposite me. He put those rope-burned hands on the table in front of him and took one fist in the other hand and cracked the knuckles, staring at them.

"What do you want to know?" he asked.

"Where *Señorita* Scorpion is," I told him.

"I'll show that card just once more," he said. "I don't know where she is."

"I guess you know why Senator Bailes was down this way," I told him.

"I'm out of touch, down here," he answered.

"It looks like this war with Spain is the real thing," I

explained. "Teddy Roosevelt's Rough Riders are going to need a lot of horses. Government's commissioned horse runners all over the country to gather in the wildest horses for the cavalry. Some enterprising young mustanger has been going below the border for his animals, and he hasn't been too particular whether they're mustangs or broke horses he brings back. Activity seems to center around the Big Bend, and it seems like none of the state officers has been very effective in checking it. The Mexican government told Washington, if they didn't send someone responsible down, it was going to raise a helluva ruckus. Even mention of war. So Senator Warren Bailes came down to see what was up with the local authorities and try to get some action out of them. He must have dug up something good. Washington had got word they'd see the end of it in a few days. The morning after he sent the wire, Bailes stepped out onto the corner of First and Main in your fair county seat, and in bulges this Scorpion on her buttermilk hoss and empties every blue whistler in her dewey right through Senator Warren Bailes."

His eyes had taken on a smoky color, and he was staring past me, almost talking to himself. "The worst part of it is, Elgera is so capable of it. I wouldn't believe it. I still don't want to. But she is so capable of it. Get her mad and she. . . ."

He lifted his head with a jerk, as if realizing the release. His eyes moved to me, and they looked even more like a sulking bull's now. He cracked his knuckles again. That irritated me somehow.

"I don't know how out of touch you are," I said. "You seem to have a pretty busy line between here and Alpine. Where's Johnny Hagar?"

I've questioned enough men to know the value of snubbing them up like that. The unexpectedness of it lifted his head again that way. The Arbuckle's started boiling over, and he got up and moved the pot off the open blaze. They'd said he was hard to rile, but there was a stiff line to his shoulders, and I wondered how much further along the fence I could push him.

"The Douglas faction, they call it," I said. "More machine, from what I hear, with Johnny Hagar county sheriff and you town marshal in Alpine, and Elgera Douglas sitting on the county board. Striker's bunch didn't have much chance in those days, did they? What is it, Owens? What did Senator Bailes find that threatened the set-up you and the Scorpion have? How is she tied into this mustang business?"

There was a tinny *clatter*. I didn't see it for a moment. Then he backed away to reveal the coffee pot overturned on the stove and all that good Arbuckle's spreading out like ink on the floor.

"Tetchy, aren't you, for a man that doesn't know anything?" I said.

"Listen." He turned to me, and he held his knuckles again. I kept waiting for them to pop. Crazy how something like that can get on your nerves. "Listen, Welles, marshal or not, you'd better go now. I don't know where Elgera Douglas is. I don't know where Johnny Hagar is. I don't know anything. You'd better go."

I scratched my head again. "Texas Stock Association. Is that the TSA brand on those cattle you're herding?"

I didn't think he would answer for a minute. "Used to be the Scorpion's beef," he said finally, wheezing a little like a man with a bullet wound. "The courts are holding her estate till this thing is cleared up. TSA is handling the beef for the courts."

"You've got a rep as a lone wolf," I said. "Like to rod your own cut. Never favored the big combines. You don't look right in this chorus, somehow. Why did you sign on with TSA?"

He was getting more and more like a bull. It came out of him with a sort of groaning sound: "Welles. . . ."

"Maybe you don't know Kelly Striker is the president of

TSA's board of directors," I told him. "I can't figure a man like you signing onto an outfit rodded by the same *hombre* who kicked you and Hagar out of the wagon the minute Elgera Douglas's support was gone. Is there something under the sougan here, Owens, or did your guts leak out when the Scorpion bought a trunk?"

"Damn you!" he yelled, and through the yell I could hear his knuckles crack again, and that was the tip-off.

He came right across the table at me. If I hadn't already started to jump up and kick the bench back away from beneath my feet, I would have been pinned beneath the table and Owens, because his lunge had tipped it over. He and the furniture crashed over onto the floor. One of his hands struck my side beneath my ribs. For just an instant I felt the awesome strength of him. I couldn't help yelling with the pain of those pinching fingers. Then I had torn loose, going on back, and he had tumbled to the floor.

He got up with blinding speed for such a hulk, and his legs were bent to jump me where I stood against the wall. Then he stopped, with all his weight thrown forward on his toes, hands outstretched, staring at the old Cloverleaf house gun in my hand.

"Really hell with the hide off, aren't you?" I said. "I guess I'd better tell you why I really came. Spanish Jack was going to send one of his own deputies, but I wanted a talk with you anyway, so he let me serve this subpoena on you. It's for your appearance at another inquest they're holding on Senator Bailes's death next Monday. Now, shall we go for our hayburners, or do you want to dig up a tomahawk?"

II

It was about sixty miles from the border to Alpine, and Butcherknife Hill lay just about halfway between. It was hotter than the hinges of hell through those thirty miles between Butcher-knife and the county seat, and my pied mare was played clear out by the time we rode in past the Southern Pacific's brick depot and cattle chutes at the end of Main. *Si Samson's Livery,* it said on the peeling sign above the big double doors of a barn on the corner of Second and Main. Si looked like a bronco-slashed hand. He was all bent over and had a painful limp, and his hair was hogged as short and stiff as the mane on Owens's dun. He stopped when he saw us, staring at Chisos Owens.

"Judas," he said.

"What do you mean?" I asked him.

"Nothing," said Si, looking down at the ground. "Nothing. You gentlemen want to stall your animals here? Looks like they need a good rub-down. Have my boy do it for fifty cents extra."

I stepped off Pie and unlashed my saddle roll from behind the cantle. Summer dust was the color of a dirty dun horse in the street, and I had the feeling that the old man was standing in the doorway of his barn and watching us till we reached the opposite side. The Alpine Lodge was a big frame building on this corner with a wooden overhang shading the sidewalk. There was the usual line of idlers. The idleness dropped off them like a kak with the cinch cut, when we passed across the porch. I was in the lobby before I heard one of the chairs scrape. The plank walk made a hollow, wooden plump that receded southward.

Owens and I cleaned up, then went downstairs to the grub house next door. *Cecile's Café,* it said, and had as strong a smell inside as most of those greasy-sack outfits you find in a border town. I forgot the smell when Cecile came out of the kitchen.

Have you ever seen nopal after a spring rain? That's how red Cecile's lips were. Eyes that gave you the same feeling as when you look into a deep pool of cool water on a blistering day. The gingham dress was stamped with blue flowers and had built-in curves. She didn't do anything as obvious as Si Samson. But I caught the momentary hesitation, about halfway down the counter toward us, as she recognized him. Then she came on.

"Chisos," she said a little breathlessly. "Haven't seen you for ages."

"Cecile?" I asked.

"Cecile Peters," Owens said. "Marshal Welles."

"How long have you known Chisos?" I asked her.

"Long time, Marshal," she told me. "Menu?"

"That's funny," I said. "When you first came in, you looked like you'd never seen anything quite like him before."

She made a little pout with her mouth, handing Owens a menu, too, but I wouldn't let it go. I put my elbows down and leaned forward, pinning my eyes on her.

"Si Samson had the same look. So did the clerk in the Alpine Lodge. What is it, Cecile? Didn't they expect Chisos was coming back with me?"

Her smile began at one corner of her lips, not all humor, something almost wistful, and built slowly, and her eyes slid around to Owens. "Maybe that's it, Marshal," she said softly.

"Bryce Wylie was the deputy Spanish Jack told me he meant to send with that subpoena," I said.

Auburn lights rippled through her hair with the negative shake of her head, and her eyes were still on Owens.

"Spanish Jack himself?" I asked her.

"I don't think even he could have done it," she said. "As a matter of fact, I don't think there is any man in Alpine who would have wanted to try and bring Chisos Owens in, except maybe Johnny Hagar, and he's not here any more."

"What were the odds on the opera seat?" I asked.

She looked at me, and the smile was full now. "As a matter of fact, they *were* making bets. The boys in front of the Alpine

Lodge were offering odds five to one against your bringing Chisos back."

It made me mad at first, to realize how I'd been used by Spanish Jack, and then, somehow, I had to laugh. I heard the cracking sound beside me. It was Owens, with his knuckles.

"All right," he growled. "How about eating?"

"I'm right sorry, Chisos. I didn't know. I wouldn't have showed you up in front of your girl this way for the world."

"I'm not his girl," said Cecile.

I glanced up suddenly at her eyes, because she and Owens were looking at each other again, and that thing was between them. I was close enough to see the color now. Blue. A deep, dark blue. Then the roots of her hair. She sensed it and turned toward me.

"What would you suggest?" I asked, tapping the menu.

"The beef stew is particularly flavorable, Marshal." It seemed deep for her voice. Then I saw her mouth was closed, and where she was looking. Tension stiffened the deep planes of muscle across Owens's back, lifting his shoulders up till he looked like he was bent over. I turned on the stool. It was Spanish Jack, standing behind us.

He was almost too handsome. He had a head of hair so black it looked blue, thick and curly as mesquite grass. Even the burnsides were curly. His skin was swarthy but so clear and fine his cheek bones under the light gleamed through it like an Indian's, and his teeth were as white as the polished bone handle on my house gun.

I jerked my thumb at Owens. "Here's your chestnut."

Jack made a little motion with one womanish hand. It gave me the sense of leaves fluttering. "Chestnut?" he said, frowning.

I looked at one of my own hands. "My fingers aren't burned, either. Did you lose any money, Sheriff?"

Jack turned to look at Bryce Wylie who had entered behind

him. The deputy was a big, kettle-bellied man in the sloppy serge vest and pants of what must have once been a pretty good suit. He packed a *buscadero* gun belt, and it *creaked* a little as he hooked his thumbs on it and pressed down heavily, shrugging at Jack. The lawman turned back, trying to make his smile at Cecile easy.

"I told you he was a salty character," he said.

"Yeah," I said, "so full of alkali my uppers are rusty. This another one of your boys?"

The smile faded as he glanced to the other side where a third man now stood. "Yes, Marshal, Jerry Hammer. A good boy. Meet Marshal Welles, Jerry."

"Gladtameetcha, Marshal," he said.

It was interesting to see how much humor he could keep out of his empty little eyes with such a big smile on his mouth. He had that rolling bulge to his heavy thighs you get in a short man sometimes, and it had split the seams out on his buckskin *chivarras*. His upper body was the same way, looking like they'd piled on the muscles till they couldn't any more, and his white cotton shirt had trouble containing him. His nose had been broken badly, and there was a deep scar the color of raw liver cutting through the greasy blue stubble of one cheek.

"You look like you've had a hard life, Hammer," I said. I might as well have reached out and wiped that smile from his lips with my hand, the way it disappeared.

Spanish Jack formed a laugh. "We'll take Owens off your hands now, Welles. Did he cause you any bother?"

"If I had a bet on it, I would've worried about it more," I said. "What do you mean . . . take him off my hands?"

I saw Cecile stiffen a little behind the counter.

"Till the inquest, of course," said Jack.

"He was never on my hands," I said. "That was a subpoena I served on him, not a warrant."

"Yes, of course, of course," said Jack.

Owens had not turned around yet. His shoulders were still hunched forward that way.

Jack looked at him. "Coming, Chisos?"

"Wait a minute, Jack," I said. "Where are you taking him?"

"To the jail," said the sheriff. "We'll hold him in custody till the inquest."

"You said Judge Kerreway is holding the inquest," I reminded him. "He's coming all the way from Marathon to do it. Is he staying with friends?"

Spanish Jack didn't want to get his feet in these oxbows, and it began to prey on him. "What are you getting at, Marshal?" he asked, a little furrow appearing between his pretty brows.

"The judge isn't registered at the Alpine Lodge," I told him. "You couldn't hold the inquest without him, could you?"

"Not exactly. Perhaps he was held up."

"I paid an extra dollar for a double at the Lodge, and I'm not going to throw that away for nothing. I think you better let Chisos Owens sleep there tonight. If there's an inquest, he'll be at it."

"I want to make sure he'll be at it," said Jack. "Come on, Chisos."

"Don't try to put this bronc' in the chute, Jack," I told him. "It's too narrow."

"I'm taking him," he said.

"Have you got a warrant, Sheriff?"

"I don't need one."

"Then you're not taking him officially?"

"I'm taking him. Come on, Chisos."

"Marshal . . . !" This last was as shrill as a maverick calf bawling for milk, coming from Cecile, and she never finished it, because Jack had stepped forward to grab Owens's shoulder and try and pull him around. Owens came around all right, more of his own volition than Jack's. After that it all went so fast I didn't rightly take everything in.

Owens's spinning motion whirled him off the stool into Spanish Jack with his head down and those bull shoulders in Jack's middle. It carried Jack backward. Jerry Hammer pulled a gun and lunged forward to whip Owens across the back of the neck while he was still bent forward.

"Well, hell . . . ," I told them, and went in on it, dragging at my own dewey. But there was Wylie. I was suddenly blocked off by his body. He got one hand around my right wrist before I had my Cloverleaf pulled free. The palm felt like sandpaper, and I thought my bones would crumble in the grip. His body carried me right back to where I'd come from. I knocked aside the stool I'd jumped off of and crashed into the counter so hard it knocked a dirty plate off farther down.

Suddenly the whole Big Dipper was inside my head, each star flashing on and off separately. I found myself sitting on the floor with my back against the counter and those sloppy serge pants in front of me and realized dimly he must have smashed me fully in the face.

He lifted a foot to kick me. I caught it in both hands and rolled to one side. The jerk took him off balance. Before he hit the floor, I was on my feet, pawing for a stool. I couldn't see very well yet. Things were still spinning, and something thick and wet kept getting in my eyes. But I caught his movement to rise. I took the stool by its seat and jammed the legs at Wylie. He howled and tried to get away. I jumped after his rolling body, jamming the legs in when his face came around again. His screams sounded like a loco horse, and I figured I'd gotten his eyes.

"Marshal . . . Marshal . . . !"

With Cecile crying like that from somewhere, I dropped the stool and spun toward the others. Jerry Hammer was probably the only man in the room who could have closed with Chisos Owens and kept up his own end. The two of them were in the middle of the room, slugging it out. Beyond them, where Owens's first lunge must have knocked him, was Spanish Jack, just getting to his hands and knees in a corner. I figured what was in his mind and was already jumping past Owens and Hammer when Jack's fingers made that fluttering motion.

He was still on his knees as I reached him. I kicked the Colt from his hand just as it cleared leather. It skidded across the floor. He dove past me, after the gun, with a hoarse shout. I had to spin around to catch him. He had his hand on the Colt again. I don't do more walking than I can help, and my heels were still pretty well spiked. Wylie's screams became puny compared to Spanish Jack's when I stamped down.

There was a *crash* from behind me like a bunch of freight cars, coming to a quick stop. Jack was through for the moment, and I turned to see. Owens had knocked Jerry Hammer across the counter, and a whole shelf full of dishes had fallen down on him. Hammer didn't get out from under the wreckage.

Owens started rubbing the back of his neck, looking at Spanish Jack where he lay huddled on the floor, holding that mangled hand and groaning, and then at Bryce Wylie, sitting against the counter farther down with his hands over his face. Finally Chisos Owens looked at me, and stopped rubbing his neck.

"Snuffy little bronc', ain't you?" he said mildly.

III

Some opera-seat argufier said there were only two things the old-time cowhand really feared—being set afoot and a decent woman—and that he'd do anything to keep from calling a spade a spade in front of the latter. That's how a bull came to be called a duke. And here was the duke again, filling the room with that switching, pawing, snorting destruction, pacing from one wall to the other, his shoulders so big and his hips so small that his hips acted as a swivel to swing his upper body from side to side every time he took a step.

"Why should Jack want to get hold of you so bad?" I asked.

Owens stopped pacing at our hotel window that overlooked Main. "I don't know."

We had left Spanish Jack and his deputies to do their own cleaning up down at Cecile's. I had some cleaning up of my own to do. My face felt like a bronco had stamped it, and it looked that way in the cracked mirror. I poured some water from the cracked china pitcher into the cracked wash bowl.

"I really didn't think Spanish Jack would buck a government man that way," I told Owens. "He must really think he's in a fancy kak, pulling a high-heel time like that."

"Jack is Striker's man," said Owens, "and Striker practically owns the Big Bend."

"They aren't bigger than the U.S. government," I said. "I suppose I could swear out a formal complaint, or call in the military, but that would snub things up too tight. I'd like to give them a little more rope. I've sent a wire to Judge Kerreway in Marathon, and, if he really hasn't been called in to sit on a second inquest, that will put a new rigging on this horse. What you got, Chisos, that they want so bad?"

"Nothing," he said. "I don't know."

"What did you think you'd find out, signing up with TSA?"

He turned to look at me. His eyes met mine in the glass. For a minute that sullen, powdery color filled them. Then I saw the pattern of crow's feet around the edges. It might have all been from weathering, or he might have been studying something. He moved over toward me, still watching my face in the glass.

"What do you mean to do . . . when you find the Scorpion?" he asked.

"My duty would be to bring her in and turn her over to the

proper authorities," I said. "How much of a chance do you want me to give her?"

He took an impatient breath, turning back. "I'm mixed up, Marshal. For the first time in my life, I'm mixed up. I've always been able to ride straight down the trail before. When things got in my way, I got them out of it in one manner or another. But I'm up against a fence here, and it's hog-tight and horse-high and bull-strong, and I can't get through. I saw her do it. I was standing right down there on the corner of Second and Main when Senator Bailes came out of the Alpine, and I saw her ride up on that palomino and empty her gun into him, and ride away."

"And you can't quite believe it."

He shook his head. "I'll believe she shot him. I know Elgera. But there's something wrong."

"Wasn't Kelly Striker the campaign manager for Bailes when he was running for the Senate?" I asked.

I saw him nod in the mirror.

I wiped my hands on the bloody towel. "I'll give the woman the same chance I gave you, Chisos," I said.

He turned again, and there were those crow's feet. "Just why did you jump in down there? You put your foot in a deeper bog than you realize. Spanish Jack won't forget it, and Striker's a big man. He might even have the power to touch you."

"I didn't like the length of Jack's burnsides," I said.

Owens laughed suddenly. It was the first time I'd heard him do it. "All right, Marshal," he said. "When I told you I didn't know where Elgera is, I meant it. But there are a few leads. That palomino of hers, La Rubia she calls it, The Blonde. Nobody else could ride it. A Mexican friend of mine claims he saw it without a rider down by the Dead Horse Mountains. That's near the Santiago Valley. Not many people could find her, if she was hiding out in her old home. I've been to the valley myself a couple of times lately and didn't come across any sign that she was there. But if you want to have a look-see, I'll take you."

"That would make me as happy as a red bangtail in a Porter kak."

Sierra del Caballo Muerto, they called them, the Mountains of the Dead Horse, because some Spaniards had got lost there in the old days, and they and their horses had all died through lack of water. I thought I'd seen some badlands in my time, but they were the Promised Land compared to this. There were trees, sometimes, but they didn't pack any more spinach than you could grow on a slick horn. There were riverbeds, but they hadn't been wet since a hundred years before the first Comanche burnt sotol stalks in rimrock. There was *toboso* grass, but it was so tough even the buffalo had let it alone.

Buzzards floated on air so still that it hurt my ears, and they must have been waiting up there a long time for us, because I couldn't see anything else alive enough to die. My pied horse was gaunted up like a heifer with the Spanish fever, and I had to get off every half hour or so and wipe the alkali out of his nose so he wouldn't choke to death.

> *There ain't no hoss that cain't be rode.*
> *There ain't no man that cain't be throwed.*

"Will you shut up?" Chisos Owens said. "There ain't no cause to sing. We're just about at the entrance to Crimson Cañon. It leads into the Lost Santiago Mine. The mine goes clean through this hogback of the Dead Horses into Santiago Valley. If you want to turn back, now's your chance. From here on it's touch and go."

"Let's go, then," I told him.

He stepped off his dun and unslung a pair of old *armitas* he had hitched to his saddle horn. He buckled these hide aprons on and got a pair of gloves from his saddle roll. I saw why in a few minutes. The cañon walls were as red as rot-gut bourbon, and so narrow we were riding in shadow dark as night at two in the afternoon.

Soon the way became so choked with prickly pear and horse-maiming cactus and mesquite we could hardly force our way through. Coming from the north, I wasn't even prepared by as much as having *tapaderos* on my stirrups. The thorny brush kept tearing my boots out of the oxbows and ripping holes in my Levi's and gouging my hands till I was ornery enough to eat horseshoes. Owens didn't pay any attention, and finally we reached the end, and, sure enough, pushing our way through the last bunch of brush, we found ourselves in the mouth of a mine.

My pied animal spooked when I tried to push her in after Owens's dun. I didn't blame the cuss much. There was something scary about that shaft. Not the fact that the beams looked ready to crumble in on you any minute. Not even the darkness that closed in blacker than sin after we'd left the meager light near the entrance. It was something else. Something an animal recognizes where a man can't. I've learned to trust in their judgment.

"No wonder the Douglas clan was hard to find," I said, more to make sure he was there than anything else. "What happened to the rest of her family? Didn't she have a brother named Natividad?"

"He's supposed to be in Mexico, trying to get help," said Owens. "A couple of her womenfolk have been seen down in the Chisos Mountains. That's my old pasture, and they have friends among the Mexicans in the back country. With the grapevine they've got down here, it wouldn't do much good for you to hunt them up. Word of your movements travels about as fast as you can, and the Chisos are just about as deadly as these mountains, if you don't know them."

"This mine is supposed to be over two hundred years old?"

"Simeon Santiago discovered it in Sixteen Eighty-One," he told me. "His engineer was an Englishman named Douglas. The shaft caved in and trapped Douglas and his wife and a bunch of *peones* in the valley. They lived there until Eighteen Ninety, cut off from the outside world."

"I know the story," I said. "And the Scorpion is supposed to be descended from this Douglas ranny."

"You sound skeptical," he said.

"It's possible," I told him.

"But not probable?" he said.

"You're a better judge of that than I am, being tied into all this so much," I told him.

"I've seen evidence."

"All right," I told him. "All I care about is Elgera Douglas, not her family history. Help me find her, and I'll even believe that Indian story about her being able to change from a woman into a real scorpion whenever she wants, if that'll please you."

He made a disgusted sound, and there was no more talk. I don't know how long it took us to stumble through that twisting, turning mine. He must have used up a pocketful of matches, trying to find our way back after we'd made a wrong turn. Finally we reached the other end. It was night by that time, and the moon was out. The shaft opened onto a hillside, and from the lip we could look down into the Santiago Valley.

It must have been five miles across to where the Dead Horses started building that purple, jagged wall again, and twice as far to transverse the length of the valley, with the mountains lifting up at either end to enclose it completely. There was water along the valley's floor, because there was a dark motte of trees making a strip a few hundred yards broad, seeming to run the complete length of the floor. Owens got down and began to squat around on the ground.

"No fresh tracks coming out of the mine," he said finally.

"Let's take a look at the house, anyway," I suggested.

He shrugged, and his Porter *creaked* as he climbed on again. The house was at the bottom of the slope, and, as we approached, I could see how the top bar on one of the big cottonwood corrals had fallen down. There was a porch around front, formed by a line of poles supporting an overhanging roof thatched with Spanish dagger. This thatching had dried and fallen through to litter the tiled floor of the porch. Moonlight came through the gaps this left and spilled like pools of yellow honey across the brown husks of thatching and the faded red tiles. Owens grunted like a tired cow, getting off his dun again. He hesitated before the big oak door. It had been painted blue once. It's a Mexican superstition about the Virgin Mary, I guess. It must have been some homemade paint, from some vegetable dye, because it was peeling off. I could see Owens's big barrel swell with the breath he took before he turned the hammered silver knob, and shoved the door open. I couldn't help stiffening up a little.

I saw his hand drop to his holstered Bisley, before he stepped in. It smelled like rotting leather inside, and of old, molding earth. Like a grave, I thought, and then almost cussed out loud at myself. I could hear him fumbling around in the dark. Light flared, and I saw it was from an old camphene lamp on a big oak center table. There was something ghostly about the tarnished Spanish helmet on the mantel of the fireplace.

"That's two hundred years old," he said.

"OK, OK," I said. "You want to flip to see who waters the horses?"

"I'd rather do it," he said. "That creek is drying up, and most of it's so full of alkali it'd eat the guts out of our nags. You'd have a tough time locating the good holes." He went out and came back in a minute with our saddle rolls, setting his frying pan and coffee pot on the table. "There's some Arbuckle's and a little bacon in my roll."

Then he left again. I could hear the *creak* of leather as he got in the hull. I could hear one of the animals snort, and then the pad of their hoofs, fading, softly dying. I stood, staring at that helmet. 200 years . . . all right, maybe it was 200 years old. I went to the table and unlashed his roll and got out the sack of coffee, and the greasy paper of bacon. Then I realized I'd have to wait until he got back with the filled canteens to make coffee. I went over to a pile of wood in the corner. It was rotten and crumbling, and must have been left here when the Scorpion hightailed it. The hearth was of adobe, running the whole length of the wall at this end of the room, with holes along it at intervals for pot fires, and iron pothooks swinging out on either side of the main fireplace. I had a blaze started in one of the pot-fire holes when I heard Owens coming back. That creek must be nearer than it had looked. The pad of hoofs stopped outside.

"Kelly?"

It was soft, and husky, from out there. It was a woman's voice.

"Yeah," I said, after the moment it took me to recover, muffling my voice with my sleeve a little. There was a *creak* of saddle leather . . . the *tap* of high-heeled boots across the tiles . . . the dry shuffle of the same boots through some of the Spanish dagger that had fallen off the overhang.

"No," I said, "don't buy that trunk quite yet. You ain't going any place but in."

She had started to whirl away, with the first sight of me. But the Cloverleaf house gun in my hand kept her from doing it. The door made a perfect frame for her. I thought Cecile had been pretty, but she didn't hold a hog-fat candle to this filly.

Tall for a girl, taller than me in the spike heels of those basket-stamped peewees she wore. The Mexican *charro* pants I'd heard so much of, fitting just as tightly as they said, with red roses sewn down the seams. The white *camisa* for a shirt, fitting the same way, tightly in the right places, tucked into a crimson sash of Durango silk tied around her waist. And the hair like taffy, or gold, or I don't know what—why try to compare it, when it's so much just by itself? I was a mite surprised by the little whip dangling from her left wrist. Unless I'd missed a detail in previous descriptions, this fancy quirt was something new for *Señorita* Scorpion.

"If you're really a scorpion," I said, "come on in and bite me."

Her eyes flashed like a gun barrel, catching the sun. I moved my Cloverleaf a little to let her know I wasn't joking as much as it sounded, and she stepped on in.

"Lay that dewey down on the table," I told her, and her fingers closed a little around the barrel of her Winchester, and then she stepped over to put it on the table. "Funny," I said. "I guess I've heard as much about that Army Colt you pack, and how good you are with it, as I've heard about your horse. And yet, according to the witnesses, this was the dewey you used on the Senator, too. What's the conundrum?"

She ran her hands down her hips like she wished the Colt was there, and then her lips twisted. "Who are you?" she said in a small, strained voice, harsh as mesquite scraping a saddle skirt.

"United States Marshal Powder Welles," I told her. "I've got a warrant there in my saddle roll. It's for the arrest of Elgera Douglas, alias *Señorita* Scorpion. Craziest alias I've ever heard. I served one on a jasper called himself Clarence the Cat once, but. . . ."

"Oh, shut up," she hissed at me, still standing stiff as a poker with those hands clawed against her legs. It struck me her eyes weren't right on me. They were looking over my shoulder. There was a loud *pop,* and I couldn't help jumping and whirling around. It was just a rotten chunk of wood, spitting its last as the fire ate it up. But by the time I'd seen that, it was too late. I was already whirling back as the crash came from the other direction. She'd knocked the lamp off the table, and there wasn't enough light left from that dying fire to put in the end of a coffin nail. I threw myself aside, figuring she'd go for that Winchester and was right. The room seemed to come apart at the seams with the sound of it. I saw the flash and heard the blue whistler go by me and on into the wall. My chivalry was worn thin, but I kept myself from firing at the flash, with an effort, and shouted at her from where I'd landed on my knees up against the wall after jumping aside.

"Honey, you'll be skylighted going through that door, and I swear I'll curl you up, if you try it."

I could hear her scratchy breathing from somewhere on the other side of the big room. The windows were shuttered tightly, but moonlight made a yellow rectangle of that open door, and she must have realized how right I was, because I couldn't hear her moving. The moonlight didn't help me any more than that, although, 'way back where I was, it was still as dark as a dirty boot. Then she stopped breathing.

I could hear it, too, the sound of approaching horses, and I took the chance and hollered at him: "Chisos, don't come in! We got your gal corralled, and she's just as liable to send you to hell on a shutter as not."

"Elgera?" It came from Owens out there in a cracked way, and then *creaking* leather as he swung off. "Elgera, are you in there?"

"Get him, Chisos," she said. "He's a marshal."

"No, Elgera." I could hear him coming toward the porch. "He's going to give you a chance. He knows there's something fishy about what's going on."

"What do you mean . . . a chance?" Her voice sounded thin.

"Give us the facts," I said. "Did you kill Bailes?"

"Think I'm a fool?"

"All right, we'll pass that up," I said. "Why did you kill him, then? What had he found out that would have spoiled your saddle?"

"Is that what you call giving me a chance?" she asked. "Answer any one of those questions, and I'd be putting my head in the noose. I won't admit killing him. I won't admit anything. Chisos, if you love me, get me out of here."

"Don't come in, Chisos," I said. "I want this straightened out before you come in."

"Elgera, I tell you, he'll do to ride the river with!" called Owens. "Won't you let us help you? You were seen by a dozen people when you killed Bailes. But you must have had a good reason. That's the only thing I can go on. What was Bailes doing? Was he mixed up with that mustang running himself?"

"What have you found out working for TSA?" she asked.

"I've got a relief man on that Butcherknife line camp who used to work for an affiliate of TSA in Kansas," said Owens. "He broke horses for this affiliate till one stove him up, and TSA pulled him down here on a job he could handle. This Kansas affiliate was one of the outfits the Army gave contracts to for broncos. The contract wouldn't let the affiliate put their own brand on the animals till they were broken. This buster says he saw more than one Mexican brand on them broomtails before he broke them."

"Is that the tie-in?" I asked her. "Kelly Striker's on TSA, and he managed the Senator's election campaign in the old days. Was Bailes really the brains behind this border-hopping mustang outfit? If you had that good a reason for killing him, sugar, you might get out on extenuating circumstances."

"Don't be stupid . . . !"

"I'm only trying to see you get your deal from off the top, blondie," I said, riled a little now. Nobody likes to be called stupid, not even an old knothead like me. "Give us something to work with, will you? I can't see a smart gal like you pulling a trick like that without a good reason, any more than Chisos can. Who was that you asked for when you first rode up? Kelly? Kelly Striker? Why should he be here?"

"He wasn't here," she said. "Chisos, if you don't get me out, I'll do it myself. You're a fool for trusting any lawman like this."

"I'm coming in, Marshal," Owens said.

"Don't, Chisos, please!" I called to him, but his boots *tapped* across the tiles, and his silhouette filled the door. I couldn't cut him down cold like that. Then the room began to rock again with gunshots.

"Damn you, Marshal!" I heard Owens shout, and he threw himself into the room from the doorway, until I heard his big body smash into the table.

"I didn't do it, Chisos!" I hollered, rising from against the wall, and he must have heard me, because there was a heavy groan and a scraping sound, and then something like a herd of buffaloes smashed into me, and I went down under the table he had heaved my way.

"Get out, Elgera, get on out!" he shouted.

The table was turned completely over on me, and I was pinned beneath it from the waist down. It had knocked my house gun from my hand, so I couldn't even cut one at the girl as her silhouette appeared for a moment in the moonlit door. When I went to get out from beneath the furniture, I began to appreciate Owens's strength. It was like trying to move a house off me. There was a stumbling, shuffling sound, and another silhouette filled the doorway, blocking out light. Owens must have heard me trying to get from beneath the table, because it looked like he turned in again. About that time my legs came free.

I tried to stand up, but my legs had been mashed up a lot, and they wouldn't support me. I fell over toward Owens, and he must have thought I was coming for him. I heard the grunt he made, launching himself. I tried to get up again and meet it, but he struck me, and it felt just like that table again. I went to the floor beneath his hot, pounding weight with the noise of a running horse receding in my ears.

"So you'd give her a chance, would you?" panted Owens, and I thought the roof had fallen in on my face. I tried to roll free of him and get a grip on his wrist so he wouldn't hit again, but he straddled his weight out over me and, rising up from the hips, that fist smashed into my face once more. I had gotten a hint of his terrible strength back there at Cecile's. Now, as he clutched at my side with a hand, I felt like the whole kak was being cinched on.

I heard the small, muffled sounds of pain I made, jerking beside him. He hit at me again, and the dark and my struggles caused him to miss my face and catch my shoulder. It sent a ringing numbness down my arm. I caught his thick neck with my good hand, clawing, grasping. He tore my hand away, twisting my arm up. I heard a noise, and a scream, and then realized it was me. Again that roof smashed down in my face. A light went on somewhere. At first, I thought it was the lamp. Then in a little thought way down inside of me, I realized there wasn't any light anywhere, really.

IV

There ain't no hoss that can't be throwed. There ain't no man that can't be rode. If you're really a scorpion, come on in and bite me.

What have you found out, working for TSA? I've found a gal in Alpine pretty as a spotted dog under a red wagon. That won't do you no good. Her hair ain't dyed. It's auburn clear down to the roots. And somebody in Alpine would recognize her, even if she did dye her hair. Wouldn't they? Don't ask me. I'm Kelly Striker. You're Kelly Striker . . . ?

That's what brought me out of it, I guess, because I couldn't be Kelly Striker. He didn't have a broken arm. I lay there, feeling the hard-packed earth of the floor against my back and staring up at the herringbone fashion of willow shoots that lay across the *viga* posts that form the rafters in adobe houses. I lay there, wondering which hurt worse, my broken arm, or my slashed face. I didn't want to move, knowing both of them would hurt more when I did. I could see it was daylight outside now. Morning, because it was still a little cool. I'd been unconscious that long?

Finally I managed to roll over and crawl to the door. My mare was cropping at some curly brown mesquite grass down-slope.

"Pie," I said, "will you come here."

The effort almost made those lights go out again. She just kept browsing. It hurt so I kept groaning with every spasmodic effort I made, crawling toward her. She lifted her head and that glass eye looked at me questioningly. *Damn you, after all we been through together, you just stand there and look like that.* "Come here." *Can't you see I need help? That Owens cuss thought he beat me to death! He'll see.* "Come here."

Finally I got to her. She shied a little, when I reached up for a stirrup leather. I don't know how long it took me to get in the saddle. I don't want to remember. I turned her upslope. It took us half the day to get through that cave. Maybe I passed out inside, or maybe it was just that dark. It was late afternoon when we reached the cañon on the other side. That fight through the thick brush choking the cut was the worst part, I guess. I lost count of how many times I was torn from the saddle. I was glad for a horse like Pie then. Any other animal would have spooked and run away the first time I fell, with all that mesquite *cracking* and *popping* and me yelling like crazy.

I knew the old Comanche Trail came through Persimmon Gap in the Santiagos and lined down on this side of the Dead Horses to the Río Grande, and, if I could reach it, there was an outside chance I'd be picked up. It was night before I got free of Dead Man's Cañon. The next time I fell off my horse, I stayed off. Somewhere 'way off I could hear a coyote yammering. It began to get cold, and I started shivering. I couldn't stop. Maybe it was more reaction than chill. Then I passed out again.

"Los muertos no hablan."

"Speak English, will you? My cow-pen Spanish don't fit this poke."

"He said the dead don't speak, *señor.*"

I looked up to see the two heads bending over me, one a big, fat, greasy pan almost lost in the shadow of a sombrero, the other a soft, tinted face with eyes as blue as the Virgin Mary color they put on their doors . . . and hair like taffy, or gold . . . or why try to compare it?—and I knew that I was unconscious.

Carretas, they call them, those big carts with solid wheels and cottonwood rails on the side. I could feel myself being lifted into it. The smell of fresh onions gagged me. I wondered how the smell could be so strong in a dream. Or maybe it wasn't a dream. But then, no human woman has a lap as soft as that. She had gotten in the cart with me and had sat down so her legs formed a pillow for my head. I could even feel the red suede of her *charro* pants.

"Oh, look at his face," she said in a soft, horrified way.

Her voice at the house had been thin and scratchy. It was

rich and full now, like running Durango silk through your hands. I opened my eyes. Her mouth was different, too, somehow—the lips riper and softer. Her whole face seemed softer. I wondered if she still wore that whip.

"Women are crazy critters," I muttered.

Her laugh was small, cutting off short, but it held something wild that clutched at me. "You're all right," she said, "as long as you can gripe like that. What happened to you?"

"Most of it happened after you left. Chisos. . . ."

"Chisos!"

"Yeah," I said.

"Oh, the fool, the fool," she murmured in a soft, husky way.

"No," I told her, "I was the fool. But now I've got you, and you're coming back with me."

She laughed again. "Yes," she said, "you've got me, but, before I go anywhere with you, you'd better get patched up a little. We're going to Avarillo's at Boquillos."

Well, all right, I thought, maybe we had better, because I didn't want to take my head off that soft lap just yet anyway, and I sort of snuggled back, and then the whole thing cut its picket pin and drifted off.

"*Señor,* I have seen plenty of rawhide in my time, and there are compadres of mine who swear on the Virgin's name that it wears better than iron, but I never saw a man made from it before. I have some horseshoe nails out in the back, and I have been discussing with myself whether you would thrive more on them than you would on this baby food my great, fat aunt insists will cure you."

I wasn't in the cart any more. I was in another adobe room, with slots for windows and hard-packed earth for a floor. The bed was made of hand-hewn oak slabs pegged together, and the covers of dirty, red wool smelled like goats had been sleeping in them. The man who wanted to feed me horseshoe nails stood beside the bed with a clay platter of some steaming hog tripe.

I've seen steers rolling in so much tallow they couldn't walk, but this jasper made them look like skin and bones. He had so many chins there was no telling where his jaw ended and his neck began. The sweat ran like grease from the creases. He had on a broad black belt, buckled up like he was trying to hold in some of the gut that slopped over it in great rolls that looked like white sausages in his thin silk shirt with the flowing sleeves. His eyes were like a bloodhound that I had seen once, big and sad and bloodshot, with that liquid look that makes you think they're going to spill out and run down his cheeks any minute. I'd worked long enough on this case, now, to know most of the people mixed up with the Scorpion, and there was no missing the gate in this corral.

"Ignacio Juan y Felipe del Amole Avarillo," I said.

"*Sí*, mining engineer *extraordinario*, archeologist *magnífico*, consultant on affairs of the heart, or whatever else you happen to require at the moment." He chuckled. "You are well informed, Marshal Welles."

"Where's the Scorpion?" I asked.

He raised fat eyebrows. "They have a saying down here, Marshal. *¿Quién sabe?* Who knows?"

"She brought me here."

"A peon and his wife brought you here," said Avarillo. "They found you on the Comanche Trail in this sad condition."

"Then I *was* dreaming," I said.

"*Sí*," he said. "Now try to get down some of this *pinole con leche*. And after that, we will dress your face again. My aunt has soaked the seeds of Guadalupina vine in mescal for three days. It will not make you handsome again, but it will heal the wounds."

"I wasn't handsome to begin with," I said. "How about that

hog tripe? I'm hungry."

"Not hog tripe, *señor,* please." Avarillo chuckled. "It is parched corn fluff and milk."

Whatever it was, I ate it. Then his big, fat aunt came in with this stuff soaked in mescal juice. She made Avarillo look like a gaunted dogie. If his cheeks were so fat they almost hid his eyes, I couldn't even see her eyes. She kept tugging at her pale-blue satin shawl and chuckling, and a different part of her body quivered every time she chuckled. It got on my nerves, somehow. Then, once, I caught a glimpse of her eyes, behind all that doughy fat. They weren't chuckling.

"Where's my dewey?" I said.

"Please, *señor,* I have not finished dressing your face. Your what?"

"My cutter, my lead-chucker, my hogleg . . . ?"

"Ah, he means his gun, my big, fat *tía.*" Avarillo grinned.

"In a safe place, *señor,*" she told me.

"Yeah?" I started to get up, but his big, fat aunt caught me by the shoulders.

"Please, Marshal Welles," objected Avarillo. "You are in no condition to excite yourself. Perhaps I should introduce you to Moro. He is my . . . ah . . . man, you might say. He is a Quill, a pure-blooded Indian of Mexico, and he is a very good card player. Come in, Moro."

Moro came in. I've seen a few Quills. There's something different about them you don't get in an Indian like a Comanche, or an Apache. It's like the difference between an oily bronco with a glass eye that's so full of the hokey-pokey he's always jumping around and you're on your guard every second, and a big fool with a streak of Quarter in him, maybe, who just sulks along till you've quit watching him, and then up and flips the kak. That was Moro. His eyes might as well have not been there for all they told. His mouth looked like somebody had cut a slit

39

in his face with the blade of the big Arkansas toothpick he carried stuck nakedly through the rawhide dally holding up his *chivarras*.

"*¿Chusa?*" he said, shuffling a pack of greasy, horsehide cards through fingers like big Fifty barrels.

"Poker's my game," I told him, "stud at that. I won't be here long enough to sit through a hand, anyway, Charlie."

"Moro," said Avarillo. "And I think you will be here, *señor*."

"When you took my wallet," I said, "did you happen to notice the U.S. marshal's badge pinned to the flap?"

"I respect the United States government, *señor*, more than you seem to think," Avarillo declared. "But if it ever came to pass that they questioned my respect, all I would have to do is step across the river, and that is all they could continue to do . . . question, if you see what I mean."

"*¿Chusa?*" repeated Moro.

"Hell," I said.

V

It was hot down there on the border. I ate a lot and slept a lot, and I must have gained some weight, because my Levi's started getting tight around the waist. I felt like a hog, getting fattened for the killing. Moro stayed in the room most of the time, trying to teach me that *chusa*, but my cow-pen Spanish didn't help much, and the only word he knew in English wouldn't bear repeating in polite society.

After about the first week they let me up, figuring, no doubt, I couldn't cause too much trouble with that cracked wing. Avarillo ran the local saloon in town. They called it a *cantina*. My room was at the back, and it opened directly onto the *cantina* itself, which was no more than a couple of round tables to drink at and a row of barrels at the back set upon a wooden rack so Avarillo could operate the bung-starters.

Avarillo walked down the row of barrels, thumping each one as he spoke. "Mescal, Marshal! It will make a cock of a capon, a bull of a steer, a stallion of a gelding. Tequila? The kick of a mule is a love tap. Pulque? One drink and a kitten thinks he is a *tigre.*"

"I'll take the bull-maker," I told him. "I need a little vinegar in my roan."

He poured me a big shot in a clay cup, nodding his head toward the outer door. There was a brush arbor to one side, and we sat at the table beneath that. Moro stood against one of the supports, idly shuffling his horsehide cards. The town wasn't much more than this *cantina* and a bunch of mud houses hung on the outside with the same scarlet *ristras* of chili you see at old Haymarket Plaza in San Antonio. We could look across the narrow gorge of the Río Grande into Mexico.

"Boquillos is a corruption of *boquilla* which means the little mouthpiece you find on a flute," Avarillo told me. "It came about because of the narrowness of the gorge here, no doubt."

"When you going to kill the hog?" I said.

Those eyebrows raised. "*¿Qué?*"

"Back in Webb County we always fattened our bacon before the slaughter," I said.

Suddenly he began to chuckle, leaning forward and looking up into my face. "Don't I fit the rôle of a benevolent host, Marshal?"

"About as well as a dun trying to look like an albino," I said.

His chuckle spread over his whole body, in waves, and he peered closer. "You know, Marshal, my big, fat *tía* . . . she thinks you are so quaint, with your cynical colloquialisms. I imagine it amuses many people . . . doesn't it? . . . so that they overlook what lies behind it. I would not like to be Chisos Owens right now. In his place, I would have rather killed you, than beaten you like that and left you alive. Perhaps Chisos does not realize it. Perspicacity is not one of his attributes. Perhaps not many people realize it, but I have always prided myself on my judge of character. I would hate to have you on my trail, Marshal." He leaned back, taking a deep breath. "We are not fattening you for the kill, Marshal. You may leave whenever you wish, my friend. No . . . ? *Sí.*"

"The Scorpion's far enough away to be out of my reach . . . in other words?"

He began to chuckle again, throwing his fat, brown hands up and shrugging. "A man's most secret thought is not safe with you around, is . . . ?" It was like somebody had noosed a California collar up tight suddenly. He almost choked on the words. Then he stood up. "We have had our appetizer. Shall we repair to the festive board now?"

But I had seen that glance past me. I got up and made to approach Moro, still leaning against the post. My good right arm was toward him as I passed, and he had just started to lean his weight forward away from the post when I did it, so casually he didn't know what happened till I had that blade out of his belt.

"I never repaired anything but a broken pack saddle," I said. "I don't think I'll start treating my victuals that way so late in life. Instead, let's you and me just move around the corner, Moro, while Ignacio here meets whoever's coming up the trail from the cañon. Make a wrong move, and I'll cut out your brisket with this Arkansas toothpick."

"It is not a toothpick, *señor,*" Moro told me, staring past us with a twisted face. "It is a *belduque,* used by the blood-drinkers of the *cordillera.*"

"Whatever it is, act natural, or you'll have some more blood to drink," I told him. "Git, now, you black Injun."

I could feel Moro twitching, with that point in his gizzard. He walked around the corner like the ground was covered with bantam eggs he didn't want to break. Avarillo stood beneath the arbor, wringing his hands and cussing under his breath in Spanish. In a minute, a jasper bulged into view at the lower end of town, coming up a trail that looked like it started at the bottom of the cañon. He was over six feet tall, gaunt without being skinny, something reckless about his slouch in the saddle. He had on a pair of old bull-hide chaps, scarred and ripped with recent brush riding, and his John B. Stetson had the Texas crease you can spot a mile away. The three-quarter rig was so sweaty even its creak was soggy as he swung off.

"Seen her?" he asked.

"No, no," said Avarillo, wringing his hands.

I could see the man's eyes now. Red-rimmed and grim, stabbing at Avarillo like nails pinning up a Reward dodger. "She was up north of Alpine last Monday," he said in a hoarse, driven way. "Busted up a mustang drive. When it was over, the horses were scattered over all of Brewster County. Half of them had Mexican brands on. Wouldn't have been known, if she hadn't scattered them that way. . . ."

Avarillo must have been making signs with those elevator eyebrows, because the man stopped suddenly, staring at the fat Mexican. I decided it was about time to intrude. I made my own signals with the point of that knife, and Moro reacted, moving around the corner.

"Leave your hands off your hardware, Sheriff Hagar," I told him. "I can cut both your ears off with one throw of this Arkansas toothpick."

"*Belduque, por favor,*" groaned Moro.

"Or should I say ex-Sheriff Hagar," I told the newcomer. "Take both your deweys out and drop them on the ground, and don't try to pull no Curly Bill spin, or I'll curl *your* bill."

He gripped the ivory handles of his Peacemakers without putting his index fingers through the trigger guards, and eased them out. There was just a fraction's hesitation. I let my wrist twitch so the sunlight ran along the knife blade. The Peacemakers made dull *thuds*.

"Step away," I told him, and then went over and picked them up, stuffing them in my belt. Then, casual-like, I flipped the knife at one of the cottonwood supports holding up the arbor. It was at the other end, some ten feet away, a thin pole at that. Avarillo looked at the blade, quivering a little in the cottonwood. Then he looked at Johnny Hagar.

"Don't you look good"—he chuckled—"still in your ears?"

"How do you know the Scorpion was up north of Alpine last Monday?" I asked Johnny Hagar.

His face was turned gray with dust, and sweat had made two glistening grooves from his nostrils to the corners of his thin, closed mouth.

I let my good hand move a little closer to one of the Peacemakers. "I could *shoot* your ears off just as well."

He drew in a thin breath. "A dozen people saw her. A couple of big ranchers . . . the station agent at Sanderson . . . Spanish Jack."

"What was Jack doing there?" I said.

Hagar shrugged. "He was called in after it happened . . . cut her sign south of Alpine . . . lost her around Butcherknife."

Avarillo must have seen the expression on my face, and it must have been going around in his mind for some time now. "Just what was the fight between you and Chisos Owens about, Marshal?"

"We had found Elgera Douglas at the Lost Santiago," I said. "He was trying to keep me from taking her back to Alpine."

Just before a norther hits sometimes, it gets as quiet as that. I don't think they were even breathing. Finally Hagar let out a disgusted breath.

"That's impossible. She couldn't have made it from Alpine to the Santiago in the same day. Not even on her palomino."

"She was there," I said.

"And she was north of Alpine," he said. "Beyond any doubt."

"One of us is lying," I said.

"There is a dead man who once called Sheriff Hagar a liar." Avarillo smiled.

"I hope he doesn't get too tetchy on that point of honor now," I said. "Seeing as how I've got the hardware."

"We seem to have reached an impasse," said Avarillo.

"If you mean, we're up against a fence, not necessarily," I said. "Finding the Scorpion might clear up this little discrepancy, as well as a few others. You seem to have been working hard trying to locate her, too, Hagar. Why is that?"

"I don't think she murdered Bailes."

"That was witnessed," I said.

"She must have had a good reason, then," he said.

"You change horses pretty quick," I said. "Is yours a reason that would stand up in a court of law?"

He shook his head from side to side like a bull with blowflies. "I don't know, but. . . ."

"I think you're in the same wagon Chisos Owens was," I said. "You're in love with the gal, and you want to ride her trail, no matter what she does. A man that dizzy over a filly ought to be willing to make a deal."

"What kind of deal?"

"Be careful, Johnny," said Avarillo.

"I took it for granted, to begin with, that Chisos Owens knew where the Scorpion was," I said. "But I don't think he'd deliberately lead a lawman onto her, the way things happened. So now, I'm taking it for granted you don't know where she is. She seems snubbed in pretty tight to this mustang-running gang. I think maybe once we find out their secrets, we'll find hers. Nobody has been able to find where they cross the border. You probably know more about this section of the Río Grande than anybody, Ignacio, from what I hear of you. How about it?"

He shrugged his fat shoulders. "The buzzard leaves no tracks in the sky."

"And a blind bronco also tears up a lot of brush on his way to the water hole," I said, "if you go in for sayings. And that's just what I'd be, wandering around down here. I'd tear up a helluva lot of chaparral before I found the sink. You can let me go on alone, if you want, but there's no telling what I'd bump into, or turn up. Wouldn't you rather be there when it happened, than not?"

Avarillo looked at Hagar. "He is right, Johnny. With a man like the marshal, it is sometimes better to help him than let him run around loose."

"If you two aren't mixed up in this mustang running yourselves, and know where they're crossing, I can't see what you'd have against showing me," I told them.

"Good," said Hagar, "but get this, Marshal. If we find the Scorpion, and you try to take her in, there isn't anything I won't do to stop you, even if I have to kill you."

VI

I'd thought that ride into the Santiago had been through the worst badlands this side of the misty beyond, but they were blue-root pastures from a mortgaged cowman's dream compared with what Avarillo and Hagar dragged me into. It all seemed connected with death, somehow, and that didn't help. Below Boquillos was Dead Man's Turn, where some grissel heel had been shot on a high ride. Beyond that was the old Smuggler's Trail with a big stone tower overlooking it that they called Murderer's Haunt because some blue bellies had been starved to death there during the War Between the States. And then on into the Dead Horse Mountains again.

"From Alpine on down," Avarillo told me, "the Santiagos

and the Dead Horses make a spine of impassable mountains with Rosillos Basin on their west side, and Maravillas on their east. The Smuggler's Trail crosses the Río Grande just east of Boquillos, and then either turns up or down, east or west. The Rangers know that this ancient trail is being used by the mustang runners, but they always turn either east or west on this side of the river, looking for them to take either the Rosillos Basin north, or the Maravillas. To their knowledge, there is no known way through the Dead Horses. It would be certain death. But that is only to their knowledge."

"And to *your* knowledge, there's a trail striking due north through the Dead Horses into the Santiago Valley," I said. "Once in the valley, they've got that creek to carry them through."

He was sitting on an Arizona nightingale that was packing as much tallow as he was, the animal rigged out with an old Mother Hubbard saddle and a spade bit with shanks as long as shovel handles. *You'd need that much leverage,* I thought, *to stop that iron-mouthed knothead.*

"Your perspicacity constantly amazes me, Marshal," he said.

"Simple geography," I said. "And I suppose you aren't the only one who knows this trail. Since it goes right into the Scorpion's home pasture, I suspect she knows of it."

The Mother Hubbard *creaked* like a rusty gate, as he leaned his weight toward me, looking sorry as grease. "You think she is running the mustangs?"

"What else does it add up to?"

"Perhaps we had better not take you through," he said.

"I could do it alone, and, if the Scorpion winds up on the end of this one, she'll find herself in Alpine faster'n a water bucket down a go-devil," I told him.

"Oddly enough," he said, "I think you could. No one else has, but I think you could. That is why we shall go on, if you wish."

I wished. Maybe I was sorry for it afterward. No trees. No brush. Not even those rings of stones you find out in the Rosillos, blackened on the inside where some Comanches had roasted *sotol* stalks maybe a century before. Just sand and rocks and creosote and sun. Pie had taken on some tallow with Avarillo's grain, but I could see it lather up and drip off her, pound by pound.

> There ain't no hoss that cain't be rode.
> There ain't no man that cain't be throwed.

"*Señor*, must you add to our misery?"

"Oh, go ahead and let him sing, Avarillo, I kind of like it." Hagar grinned as he said it. I'd heard about that grin, too, and how nothing short of the devil could wipe it off, and maybe not even him. I began to appreciate it farther on, when I couldn't even sing. That was when we found the first dead mustang.

We had turned north, away from the Río Grande into those Dead Horses. I don't know how many miles it was up off the river. I'd lost count. I know we'd started at daybreak, and it was now late afternoon. Hagar was leading us on his apron-faced horse, and it shied suddenly in a weary, reluctant way. I saw it, then, lying beyond some creosote bushes, and had to haul up the ribbons on my own piebald to keep her from spooking. The buzzards had been at the carcass, but the brand was still evident on the flea-bitten hide.

"*La Reja*," said Avarillo. "That is quite a big outfit in Mexico."

"Looks like it's been dead a long time," I remarked. "We're not on a fresh trail."

"No?" murmured Avarillo. The way he said it made me look at him. But he'd already turned that mule away and started on up the cut.

We lined deeper into the Dead Horses, stark peaks all around us. Then the sun went down, and it was darker than the inside of a ramrod's yannigan bag. Finally the moon came up as fat and yellow as a Webb County pumpkin, and its light turned the country into the kind of a picture a ranny sees after painting his nose all night. Sometimes the hogbacks turned red as the tops of a kid's Hyers; next they might be as green as wheat grass in spring with big, purple rocks poking out like post-oak bumps on a brush popper's legs.

"All right," said Johnny Hagar abruptly, and swung down off his dun. We'd been traveling across shale ground, but now we had struck a strip of sand, and it was all churned up like a band of stuff had been run through here. There were droppings, too. Hagar toed some. "Fresh enough," he said. "Push a little, and we might tie into them."

Pie was so played out I had to keep giving her the boot. We crossed a saddle between two peaks and on the opposite slope saw the haze, swimming atop the next row of hills. We flagged our kites at a hard gallop down the slope and up the next. Just before the ridge, Hagar stepped off his horse and moved to the top on foot, squatting down when he reached it, to keep from being skylighted.

"Sure enough," he said. "Big bunch of them, fogging through that next valley. Looks like a full band of riders. . . ."

Maybe it was in the way he stopped. He could have ended it there, all right. But his voice sounded like a tight dally snipped off suddenly. His whole lean body stiffened, and he started to turn toward us, still squatted down like that, then wheeled back, and finally, rising at the same time, turned back toward us.

"Don't do it, Hagar," I said. "Is she down there?"

No telling what makes a man hesitate in a moment like that. Whatever it was, it gave me the chance to thwart his original intention. He had the look of going for his guns, although his hands did not actually move. I can't figure him backing down on a draw out, even though in his moment of hesitation his glance was pinned on my own hand, close enough to that Cloverleaf in my belt. At any rate, I had already booted my horse up, and by the time he went into his final move, faced toward me, I was close enough to ram my horse in against him, knocking him off balance.

"Marshal, I told you . . . ," he gasped, grabbing for my bridle.

But I was on the crest, then, and could see down into the next valley. A bunch of mustangs was being run northward beneath a dirty-brown mist of their own dust. There were two riders dragging, one on swing, and one on point. I couldn't make out what color their horses were exactly. But there's one color you can't miss, even under those conditions. It's that pale gold tint of a true palomino, set off by the pure white mane and tail. And there it was, outriding, on the opposite slope, and the rider had hair as blonde as the horse's.

Hagar had the shank of my bit in one hand now, and his tug caused Pie to whinny and rear up. I necked hard to the right, swinging the animal around into him by its rump, and freeing one foot from the stirrup at the same time. My boot caught him under the chin. He made a sound like a roped dogie when it hits the ground, and the sudden release of his hold on my bit caused Pie to plunge forward. Hagar was falling over backward, and I had swung out my stirrups to kick the horse on over the hill, when Avarillo's voice came from behind me, soft and bland as hog fat dripping down a candle.

"Not quite now, Marshal, if you please."

Any other man, I might have gone on and kicked Pie over the hill. But there was something in his voice that made me turn around, still holding my feet out. I don't know where he'd gotten the stingy gun. It was a little four-barreled Krider pepperbox almost hidden in his fat hand, but at this range it would be deadly.

"I'm going on over, Avarillo," I told him. "She's down there, and I'm going to nail her this time, and nobody is stopping me. If you want to open my back door, go ahead."

I turned my back on him. I didn't make the mistake of hustling over the crest. I dropped my feet in easy, heeling Pie into a deliberate walk. Hagar lay on the ground, watching in an unbelieving daze. Then I was over the top and going down the other side.

Once beneath the crest I pushed Pie into a gallop down the steep talus, praying for the sure feet she'd shown so many times before, giving her a free bit and letting her slide, when she wanted. I was right on the flank of the band and quartered in, meaning to drop behind the drag riders and pick up the girl on the other side. But I didn't use enough cover, I guess. They must have caught sight of me coming down. Somebody started gun racket.

I couldn't hear any of those blue whistlers, whining my way, or see them kicking up dirt around me, but the gunshots came from down there somewhere. It was a case of dive right on in or duck, and I wanted that girl too much to turn my tail.

"Git on there, you piebald cousin to a rat-tailed ridge runner!" I howled at Pie, and she really lined out under that, because she knows I never yell at her unless I really want to shovel on the coal. The gunshots mingled now with the sound of running horses to deafen me, and the dust billowed up to gag me, and I raced around the drag end of that band of pepper-gut broncos. A horsebacker bulged out of the blinding dust ahead. He was turned the other way in the saddle with his Winchester, and it surprised me. He jerked around my way, when he saw me coming, looking as surprised as I was, and pulled his rifle over the saddle bows.

I cut loose with my Cloverleaf, shooting at his horse. I saw his hat twitch off, and that's how accurate you can be on a running animal with a six-iron. His Winchester made its bid then. I saw it buck across his saddle bows and saw it reach out with that red finger. I could feel Pie jerk against my legs. *Damn you, if you've dusted my horse,* I thought, and squeezed my trigger again, kicking my feet free of the stirrups at the same time. Pie went head over heels, and I threw myself clear, trying to roll it off.

But the ground was rocky, and my broken arm caught it. I heard myself bawl like a roped heifer, and then went flopping off across rocks as sharp as a razorback hog, howling and grunting before coming to a stop against a boulder.

I lay there a minute, spinning like a trick roper's Blocker loop. I could hear somebody groaning. It was me. When I realized that, I knew I was beginning to come out of it. My busted wing hurt even worse than the first time it had been snapped. The thunder of running horses had faded into the distance, and the gunshots were farther off, too, not coming so hot and heavy now. Then I began to hear that other sound. It was like something scraping over rocks. It *was* something scraping over rocks.

"Jerry?" called someone. "Was that you going down?"

I had cover on one side from the boulder. I could see my Cloverleaf, lying out in the open where I'd dropped it. I had to make a quick decision, and decided I'd rather check out, making some kind of bid, than just sit here and wait for them to rake the pot in. I rolled over on my belly and began snaking toward my iron. I was within a couple of feet of it, when that scraping sound stopped, and it was the soft, gritty noise of boots stepping into sand. My fingers were an inch away from that Cloverleaf-shaped cylinder on my Colt house gun, when he spoke from behind.

"Don't do that quite yet, Marshal. I want to enjoy this a while before I send you to hell on that shutter you unhinged for yourself back at Cecile's."

I stayed in that position a minute, or a year, I don't know. Then I twisted my head around, with my hand still pawed out that way, so I could see him. I had already recognized his voice, of course.

"Well, Bryce," I said, "light down and give your horse a rest."

There was a small, puckered scar in the flesh of his cheek, like someone had punctured it with something, and he wore a black patch over one eye. He passed the palm of his free hand over that side of his face, without actually touching it, and his lips pulled away from his teeth in a flat grin.

"I've been waiting for this, Marshal," he said. "You don't know how long I've been waiting for this. You don't know how I've thought and dreamed and planned this moment. I never hoped to have the drop on you, of course. I thought it would have to be flip, cock, and shoot, and all the pleasure would have to be after you was dead. This is so much better.

"Start squirming, Marshal. I'm not going to kill you right off. I'm going to shoot you in the legs, so you can't move away, and then in the belly. That will take a long time. Hours . . . maybe even a day or so. With your tripe leaking out the hole, Marshal, and the sun coming up and burning you like a match roasting a fly. Ain't you going to beg, Marshal? If you beg a little, maybe I'll let you off easy."

I began to sweat. I couldn't help that. I didn't figure he'd be so nice as to put out my bull's-eye quick, even if I did squall. The only thing I could hope would end it fast was if I took a quick grab for my gun and made him take a snap shot. He couldn't be as certain that way, and there was an outside chance it might snuff my candle then. Two pair against a straight, but there weren't any more draws left in this game for me. My whole body stiffened. He must have seen it. He cocked his .44.

I decided I might as well step in the kak, now as any time, and reached out for my Cloverleaf. I never heard a gun go off louder. My whole body jerked so tightly I cried out with the shock it sent through me. But somehow I could still get my fingers around the walnut grips of my own gun, and I turned over on my back with it in my hand.

Bryce Wylie was standing on his toes. He was looking down at them. Even his gun was pointed at his toes. There was a sick look on his face. Then, slowly, still hanging there like he was in a California collar, his left hand reached across and spread out over his belly. His gun dropped out of his right hand, and he pitched over on his face.

As I lay there, staring at him, it came to me that I felt no pain, that it was not Wylie who had shot at all. I rolled over on my belly and helped myself onto my knees with my good hand.

"Well," I said, "if you aren't the shootin'est gal I've ever seen."

"You've got a lot of sand in your own craw, Marshal," the Scorpion said, coldly blowing the smoke from the end of the big Army Colt she held and stuffing it back into the holster.

Her hair shone like wet gold. Her bottom lip was ripe as 'possum berries in the spring, and the shadow beneath it made her look like she was pouting. And now was the time to wear a whip, but she didn't have one.

"Saving my life that way sort of complicates matters," I told her. "I really meant it when I said I was going to take you in, Elgera."

It's funny, the shine blue eyes get sometimes.

"Before you even heard my side of the story?"

"I'm listening."

"What would that behind you indicate?" she said.

"That I was cussed lucky you came along just then."

"Not lucky. I saw what happened from the other slope. But I don't mean that. Doesn't Wylie and Jerry Hammer's connection in this mean anything to you?"

"They're Spanish Jack's men," I said.

"And Jack is Kelly Striker's man," she said.

"You mean the TSA?" I asked her.

"You're a government man," she said. "Couldn't you have a government auditor go over their books?"

"They're shaky?"

"It would be my bet that TSA is in as much red ink as they are in blood," she told me. "Why should a big corporation like that contract to handle my cattle for the courts till this thing is cleared up? What they make off that would be chicken feed compared with what they get handling beef they can drive to market."

"Maybe you're working for Striker, too," I said. "So when Bailes finds out TSA is pulling a fast one, he has to be eliminated, and Striker picks you for the job."

"That's not very logical," she said, and I could see the flush beginning to tint her face that colored her words. "Kelly Striker has been bucking me in Brewster County for years."

"It's not very logical that you would shoot Chisos Owens back at the Santiago and then save my life, either," I said.

"Chisos!" Now I could see the color seep out of her face. She bent toward me, letting it out in a heavy breath. "Where? Where is he, Welles?"

"You ought to know better than I," I told her. "When I came around back in your house, he was gone, too. I figured he'd taken out after you."

"After me? What are you talking about?"

"At the Santiago," I said. "That Monday. What had you done . . . just run another band of these pepper-guts through?"

That buttermilk horse of hers stood a few feet behind her, and she began to back toward it. Her eyes were shining slits in her face. "You're trying to forefoot me. I wasn't at the Santiago on any Monday since Bailes was killed. Chisos isn't shot."

"You ought to know," I said. "But all that blood on the floor at the Santiago wasn't mine. I think you gut-shot him good, and he's either holed up somewhere or dead . . . somewhere."

"It's the same thing that happened in Alpine," she muttered.

"What happened in Alpine?" I said.

"I wasn't there."

"You weren't there when?"

"Marshal. . . ." She was bent toward me now, hands closing into fists. "Tell me the truth. Chisos isn't shot."

"I think he was," I said. "A blind greener couldn't have missed, the way he was skylighted in that door."

"Where is he?" she said.

"I don't know, Elgera," I said.

She started backing toward her horse again. I got the idea it wasn't what she had meant to do at first.

"Don't spook now," I told her. "Chisos's not here to throw you a clothesline, and I'm not losing you this time, Elgera. I try to remember what my ma taught me about being a gentleman, but I swear I'll forget every word she said . . . Elgera!"

She had whirled to that horse. I had never seen such a mount. The Mexicans teach their animals to whirl outward, but this buttermilk nag spun toward the girl as she jumped into the air. Her left toe caught the stirrup, and the inward pinwheel of that animal slapped her into the saddle faster than I could follow. She drove the palomino right at me. But I was all horns and rattles now, I was so mad, and, instead of jumping out of the way, I let that pale, writhing chest hit me. It knocked me aside, but I was still in close enough to grab her leg as it went past me, and that kept me from falling.

The palomino wasn't in its full gallop yet, and my weight, tugging on the animal, pulled it down. Shouting something, the Scorpion tried to kick free, but I slid my grip on up her leg till I had my hand hooked in that Durango sash around her waist.

With the horse still going forward, the force of it pulled her back. She lost balance and came out of the saddle and on top of me. The fall stunned me. She kicked free and rolled off, trying to gain her feet at the same time. I rolled after her, with my left wing still out of commission. For just an instant we were face to face, still on the ground. My right arm was on the upper side, and I snaked it out and grabbed her left wrist, twisting her left arm around behind her in a hammerlock.

I was right up against her, with her breath hot in my face, so close I could see the little devils dancing in her eyes. She made another violent attempt to break free. I shoved that twisted arm farther up her back. She gasped with the pain and twisted around, shoving herself hard up against me to ease the pressure.

"All right," she panted in a final, despairing defeat, "all right."

"It better be," I said, without relaxing my hold. "Now are you going to be a good girl, or am I going to have to take you back to Alpine trussed in a lariat?"

"I'll be a good girl, Marshal," she breathed scathingly, facing away from me now. "I'll be a very good girl."

Maybe it was the husky emphasis she put on the last words. Maybe it was that heat in her voice. I don't know, but it struck me for the first time how tightly she was up against me, her backside pressed against my groin. I'd thought about her a lot before now, of course. A man couldn't help thinking about a thing like that on a case like this . . . from the beginning, from the very first story . . . a woman they called *Señorita* Scorpion, and then through all the other stories . . . and coming up against men like Chisos Owens and Johnny Hagar, ready to die just for another look at her . . . and then seeing her that first time at the Santiago, and thinking about it after that. But I didn't think about her now, and that was funny, after it had been on my mind so long . . . about her. Nothing at all was in my mind now. I didn't have any consciousness of what I was doing until she turned around again, slowly, as I let go of her arm. Then I felt the ripe, soft richness of her lips against my own.

I never will know how long it lasted. Finally it was I who pulled away. She stood there, taking slow, deep breaths, staring at me. Her eyes weren't half closed in that sleepy way any more. They were staring at me in a strange, wide surprise.

"Somehow," she said in a husky whisper, "I hadn't thought of you . . . like that."

"I'd thought of you," I said. I could hardly get it out, my throat was so drawn up. "I've got no right . . . you're my prisoner . . . and I've got to take you in . . . and they'll probably hang you. But I can't help it."

The focus of her eyes changed for a second, not seeming to be on my face now. Then the expression on her face changed, too.

"Powder?" she said in that husky way, and brought her lips in again.

I took it. Then I felt the stiffening of her whole body against me. Her arms slid along my sides and hooked around behind me, pulling me in. I tried to jerk my head back and get free of that grip, but I'd got the gate open too late. The whole state of Texas hit me on the back of my skull, and my head exploded and scattered pieces all over Mexico, and the Dead Horses opened up and swallowed me.

VII

I've been waiting for this a long time, Marshal . . . Chisos shot? . . . I tell you I wasn't at the Santiago. I'm going to shoot you in the legs, and then in the belly . . . ain't you going to beg, Marshal? So long since I held a woman. Somehow, I hadn't thought of you . . . like that.

"If you don't stop talking so deliriously, Marshal," said Ignacio Juan y Felipe del Amole Avarillo, "you will not only reveal the details of your love life, but all the secrets of the United States government as well."

I opened my eyes to see him sitting, cross-legged, beside me, puffing calmly on a cheroot, his Arizona nightingale cropping at creosote behind him. It was daylight. I really doze a long time when they snuff my bull's-eye. Then I saw another animal working over the creosote beyond Avarillo's.

"Pie," I said, starting to rise up, and that was about as far as I got, before the back of my head seemed to split open.

He pushed me back down with a fat hand. "I thought the man with the Winchester had shot your horse, too, when I saw you go down from where I was on the hill. But evidently the animal only stumbled in that rough ground."

I rubbed the back of my head. "Hagar?"

"It was Hagar who hit you from behind," said Avarillo. "Then he and the girl headed northward. My mule cannot keep up with that palomino of hers when she pushes it. Or perhaps even my dubious scruples would not allow me to leave you here to die."

I got up finally, trying not to cuss out loud. Once was bad enough. But twice, like this, struck a man's pride. Then my eye fell on Bryce Wylie's body, over by the boulder. It didn't seem to bother Avarillo.

"I got an idea from the gal, if nothing else," I said. "I can't figure Wylie and Hammer running these mustangs on their own. If Spanish Jack is behind this border hopping, that leaves two possibilities. Either he's working for himself and double-crossing Striker, or he's working for Striker."

"And if he's working for Striker, that would bring in TSA," said Avarillo.

"Chisos said something about an affiliate of TSA in Kansas handling a lot of these Mexican broncos," I muttered. Then I lifted my head a little. "I wonder what Striker's reaction would be, if we showed up in Alpine with Bryce Wylie's body?"

We found out. I hadn't expected Avarillo to come with me really, when I said it, but he came anyway. We corralled Wylie's horse where it had run a couple of miles from the scene of the ruckus, and tied his body across the saddle. The trail took us through the Santiago, and we reached there about sundown, finding the house deserted and no fresh sign. We went out through the cave that night, and up to Butcherknife, where we spent the night in the empty line shack there. TSA evidently hadn't gotten around to putting another man on those cattle. We reached Alpine by early afternoon of the third day.

We rode down the middle of Main, leading Wylie slung across his horse, head down. I went near enough the curb, passing Cecile's Café, to see in through the dusty panes of the front window. It wasn't very busy this time of day. There was only one other customer besides Spanish Jack. Jack was holding Cecile's hand and leaning across the counter, and I could see those chalky teeth of his shining in that smile from where I was.

He didn't see us pass, but there was a crowd gathering around our horses as soon as I stopped them in front of Si Samson's stable. The coroner came over in a few minutes, a fat, pompous little busybody with a carnation in the buttonhole of his funeral-colored fustian. He took charge of the body, and I went over and sent a couple of wires at the telegraph office.

From the telegraph office, I saw Spanish Jack come out of the café and cut across Main toward the coroner's. Avarillo wanted to clean up first, but I dragged him, tired and dusty and pouting like a child, to the café. Cecile was behind the counter, when we came in, and gave me that smile, but somehow it wasn't the same after the Scorpion.

"You look tired, Marshal," she said.

"Big job of work about done," I said, sitting down and shoving back my hat to rub my eyes.

"About done?"

"Judge Kerreway never did come in for that second inquest, did he?" I asked.

She shook her head, watching me.

I hooked a menu and studied it. "He'll come in now. I just sent him a wire. This thing's ready to bust apart at the seams, and a lot of interesting yaks are going to pop out, when it does, including most of them connected with TSA."

"TSA?"

"Yeah. Give me some of that beef stew, will you? What're you having, Ignacio?"

"If you have it," he told Cecile, but looking at me, "I'll take a big, stiff jolt of tequila."

She wasn't as talkative as she was that first time. After she brought stew for both of us, she went back to the kitchen, and Avarillo poked me in the ribs with his elbow.

"If it is true that a closed mouth catches no flies, Marshal," he said, "you must be choking to death on them by now."

"I just thought it was about time we stirred up a little activity," I told him. "I'm getting tired chasing around all over Texas after the jaspers mixed up in this murder. It's about time a few of them came to me."

They did. They came in the late afternoon. Avarillo and I had a double at the front end of the Alpine Lodge's second story, and, waiting by the window, I saw the three horses pull up to the hitch rack below. Spanish Jack forked a shiny black with four white socks that looked like it had more flash than bottom. He swung out of his silver-mounted saddle with a flourish. Jerry Hammer climbed off his copper-bottom Quarter animal with as little effort as possible. I had never seen the third man before.

"I think Kelly Striker's come to pay us a visit," I said. "You got that stingy gun of yours?"

"But of course," he said, chuckling. "One does not travel without one's friends."

There was a knock on the door after a time. I opened it and let them in. The one I had never seen before was standing in front of Hammer and Spanish Jack. He was a big man, pompous as a grain-fed steer, shoving his gut out and planting his custom Hyers wide apart, so you couldn't miss how important he was. The flesh of his face looked like inch-thick rare beefsteak, and his bloodshot eyes had gazed down the neck of a lot of good bottles. And yet, somehow, they held a little glow in them, and I got the idea the results of rich living only hid what was beneath.

"Kelly Striker," he said officiously, introducing himself. The two words sounded like somebody shoving a pair of .44 flat noses home in the cylinder of a Colt. "I would have made your acquaintance sooner, Marshal, but you left in such a hurry last time."

"Business," I said. "Maybe you'd like to hear about your man?"

"Spanish Jack's man," Striker corrected me, stepping in as I moved back.

"Oh," I said. "You've just come along for the ride?"

"I hold a natural interest in what goes on in Alpine," he said. "What *did* happen to Bryce Wylie?"

"I came across him blotting some brands off TSA beef down by Butcherknife," I told Striker. "He wanted to make it a corpse-and-cartridge occasion. He did."

A little muscle twitched beneath that beefsteak flesh of his cheek, and he couldn't control the momentary, instinctive shift of his eyes around to Jack. The sheriff couldn't hide his surprise, either. Striker's glance rode back to me. He pulled back his coat to shove his thumbs behind the cartridge belt crossing his pin-striped pants, and thrust his gut out farther, walking to the window and staring down into the street.

"I can't feature that, somehow," he said. "Wylie was making a hundred and fifty a month as a deputy. Why should he risk his job for a few rustled beeves?"

I didn't answer. Avarillo was sitting on the bed, staring at me in a puzzled way. Jerry Hammer leaned against the door frame, building himself a smoke. I felt like a hide pinned to the wall with those empty, unblinking, little eyes on me.

"Are you sure?" said Kelly Striker, putting so much pressure on his gun belt with those thumbs that it *creaked*. He turned back to me. "Are you sure this didn't just happen on the road somewhere? Wylie wasn't the kind to forget what you did to him at Cecile's."

"Wasn't he?" I said.

Striker took a heavy, labored breath like a horse that had lost its wind. "A public officer shot a man down in Duval County about six years ago over a personal affair like that, and it caused him quite a lot of trouble. A mob wanted to hang him. He was put on trial. He was acquitted, but they removed him from office, and he had to leave Texas."

"Folks don't mind a man doing his duty," said Jack, shifting his weight from one leg to the other like a fiddling stud. "But when he uses his office to settle personal differences. . . ."

He was a high-strung man to begin with, of course. I wondered if he was this nervous all the time, though. I found the tail of my eye on those womanish hands of his, waiting for that fluttering movement.

"Yes," interrupted Striker, "Wylie was well liked around here, Welles. If it got to drifting around that things had happened that way, I'm afraid it wouldn't go so well with you."

"You seem to be working up some kind of beef," I said.

"I'm only interested in the welfare of this community," he

said. "Mob violence is a terrible thing. Even if it wasn't a personal grudge between you two, Washington might question the affair rather closely, if the wrong kind of rumors reached them. Now I have no doubt it happened just the way you said. But for your own protection, Marshal, I think it would be wise to retire. I have connections in Washington. It could be done with no taint on your record. We could just move you onto another job, and get a fresh marshal out here."

"No," I said, "I can't see it that way. I'm too close to cracking this thing. I've got too much evidence another marshal couldn't use the way I can. It's going to bust higher than a broomtail hauling hell out of its shuck, Striker. It's going to shake a lot of men loose from their kaks."

Striker took another hoarse breath. "Won't you reconsider?"

Hammer had a last puff on his coffin nail, dropped it to the floor, ground it beneath a heel. Then he straightened from where he had leaned against the frame. The bedsprings *creaked* as Avarillo bent forward slightly. Jack's hands were motionless, at his sides.

"No," I said, and became conscious of the hard, cold feel of my own dewey against my belly. "I'll finish the ride."

"Oh?" said Striker. That little glow flared in his eyes.

I couldn't help keeping tabs on Jack's hands. I took in a breath and held it.

"Oh," said Striker again, and turned and walked out the door, and Jack and Hammer wheeled, and followed him.

VIII

Lights began to poke yellow holes in the evening along Main Street. Si Samson's livery doors groaned as he swung one shut against the rising chill. I stood at the window, hearing the *creak* of saddle leather as Striker and his boys mounted in front of the hitch rack below. Striker swung off north toward his home in the hills out there. Jack and Hammer trotted their animals around onto Second and out of sight. The jail was over there.

"I thought for a moment they were going to make a play," said Avarillo, still sitting on the bed. His eyes dropped to the walnut handle of my Cloverleaf. "They say Jack is a dangerous man. Even Hagar has a healthy respect for him."

"I've got his number," I said.

Avarillo chuckled. "I was beginning to lose my faith in you, when you talked like that in Cecile's. I think now, however, I perceive a pattern. You thought she would pass it on?"

"Didn't you see Jack sparking her when we passed?" I asked.

"And you think Striker found out what was in that wire you sent?"

"I hope he did," I said. "TSA has their headquarters in Waco. That's where I sent the wire. I asked the marshal's office to dispatch a government auditor to check over TSA's books. The Scorpion gave me that idea. If Striker did have the influence to find out what was in the wire, and TSA's books are shaky, I figured it would put a bee in Striker's bonnet."

"His sombrero was buzzing pretty loudly when he came here," said Avarillo. "But why didn't you tell him where you really found Wylie?"

"He would know where I stand," I replied. "This way, he might figure I'm lying about Wylie, and that I really found Wylie with those mustangs and suspect Wylie's connection. But he isn't sure. He's confused. Have you ever seen a steer when it's confused? It gets boogered and stops figuring its moves. Then you can haze it just about anywhere you want. I figure we've hazed Striker right into our Blocker loop."

We had. We went downstairs and sat in the lobby of the Lodge where I could look out on Second Street. There was a Mexican *cantina* next door to the jail. In about fifteen minutes, Jerry Hammer came out and unhitched his own copper-bottom and

Jack's stockinged black, leading them across to Si Samson's stable. He came out of the stable and went back to the jail. The lights in the front room of the jail went off in a minute. We went out and crossed Main, going between two houses on the opposite side of the street to an alley behind. There, under a cottonwood, we waited. In another ten minutes, Hammer came up the alley farther down and went in the back door of the livery barn. He came out, riding his own horse and leading Jack's.

"A childishly elaborate plan to deceive us," said Avarillo at my side, and chuckled. That chuckle shook his kettle gut. "When do we get our horses, Marshal?"

"Right now," I said.

Si Samson came out of the little room he had up front, when we hit the barn, scratching his roached mane and grumbling. "More damn' horses coming and going than I ever seed in Alpine before."

"Just got word Chisos Owens is gut-shot and dying down in the Santiago," I told him.

He looked at me with a strange, tight expression, then snorted, and turned back up the aisle to get our horses. Avarillo sighed heavily.

"What new, diabolical plan has the mad marshal in mind?"

"What do you figure the Scorpion would do, if she found out Chisos Owens was dying somewhere?"

"Go there," he muttered.

"That's what I figure," I said. "The way the grapevine works around here, she ought to hear about this before we get out of town."

Even his smile was fat. "It is surprising how fast word can travel in such a desolate country. But then, most of the people are her friends. But why the Santiago?"

"When the Scorpion first came on me down there in the

house, she asked for Kelly, before she saw me," I told him. "They had made it a meeting place."

Si brought back our horses. We filled our canteens at the water trough outside, then headed north out of town, past the cattle chutes at the railroad yards. I didn't bother trying to track Spanish Jack and his deputy, figuring they would meet somewhere near Striker's house. We topped the first rise and saw them in the light of a rising moon about a half mile ahead. Striker's home hunkered in a big grove of trees off the road at the crest of the next hill. A horse was coming down the road from there. It met Jack and Hammer at the wooden bridge crossing Calamity Creek in the cut. They all headed south, around town and on down toward Butcherknife.

The road followed Calamity Creek down to where it turned west just above Butcherknife Hills, the road bending east toward the Santiagos then, away from the creek. It was the only main route south, and we didn't bother keeping Striker and the others in sight, just trailing behind them most of the time, but checking up on their tracks once in a while and traveling the brush beside the road in case he sent one of his boys back to see if they were being followed.

We followed Chalk Draw down into where Crimson Cañon opened out, and then into that red cut, with its brush so thick that every foot was a battle. We could see by the moonlight and star shine indication where Striker and the others had forced their way through ahead of us—mesquite berries newly torn off their brush and recent horse droppings in the decay underfoot.

It was nearly dawn when we reached the end of the cañon. The brush thinned here, and the cañon opened up into sort of a bowl. The mouth of the mine was on one side of the bowl, so covered by tangled chaparral and devil's head that no one would suspect it was there if they didn't know about it.

One of the ears on Avarillo's mule flopped toward the cave.

"*¿Qué pasa, querida?*" he asked the critter.

"You cover me," I told him, getting off with as little noise as possible. "Striker might have left one of them behind."

I snuggled around the outside edge of the bowl, keeping in as much brush as possible, till I reached the mouth of the mine. There I could hear what the mule must have. It was a heavy, labored sound, like someone breathing. It stopped, after a minute. It took me a long time to get through without making any noise. With the last bit of brush still screening me from the inside of the mine, I could see him. Dim light from the sky filtered through to reveal his body stretched out, face down on the floor.

"I got my dewey on you, Hammer," I told him. "If you're dealing one from the bottom, you'll get your lights put out."

He made an effort to lift his head, failed, groaned heavily.

I crawled out with my lead-chucker pointed at him. Crouching beside him, I turned him over. It looked like a whole herd of Texas longhorns had walked across his face. I had never seen such a bloody mess. His shirt was ripped down off his chest, and I got a good look at those muscles. They were like thick slabs of quilting covering his body, and one shoulder was bared like half a Webb County cantaloupe.

"It must have been about ten men," I said.

"Owens." It was hard to understand him through his smashed lips. "Chisos Owens. Striker left me to guard this end of the cave. Owens came through like you did. I tried to stop him. . . ."

"Like trying to stop a stampede," I said.

He didn't answer, and then I saw he had passed out. I went back and got Avarillo. We loaded Hammer on the rump of his mule, head down, and started picking our way through that shaft.

IX

There is no measuring time in a place like that. When we reached the other end, the first dawn light was beginning to silhouette the jagged outline of the Dead Horses across the valley. The windows of the house still in shadow made yellow rectangles against the darker shape of the walls. We left our animals hitched to the corral 100 yards behind the house, stretching Hammer out on the ground and tying his hands for good measure.

"Perhaps one of the shutters in back can be forced," suggested Avarillo.

Two wings of the house stretched out on either side of a flagstone patio, with poplars growing around a dried-up well in the middle. We tried three windows along the south wing before a shutter gave. It was a bedroom, with a big four-poster at one side. I got my face full of cobwebs, climbing through. The door led to the hall. Cat-footing down this, we could begin to hear voices from the living room.

"Now wait a minute, Owens," said Kelly Striker, "you're taking too much for granted."

"On the contrary," said Owens. "Judge Kerreway wasn't going to sit on any second inquest, because there wasn't going to be any inquest. Powder Welles wondered why Jack issued that phony subpoena on me. I think I know why, Striker. You'd found out I was working at your Butcherknife line camp, and you were scared I'd uncovered something, and you wanted to stop my mouth. Well, you were right, on all counts. Too bad TSA is such a big organization. You can't keep your thumb on every department. Like Waco, for instance, where I signed on as Timothy Evans. They sent me to Butcherknife. And I did uncover something. A lot of things. There's another name on your Waco payroll sheet. Sam Skee. He used to work for a Kansas affiliate of TSA. They were handling those rustled Mexican broncos."

"I can't believe it," said Striker. "If what you say is true, TSA will take the necessary measures. . . ."

"Measures, hell," said Owens. "TSA knew exactly what was going on. Sam was busted up by one of them broncos, and drinks when it gets to hurting him, and talks when he drinks. He says there was a TSA brand inspector on the Kansas company's corrals seven days a week. The inspector was working hand-in-glove with a colonel in the Quartermaster Corps who got a cut for not looking when they blotted the Mexican brands out with the Kansas company's mark."

Avarillo and I had now reached the end of the hall. The door here was partly open, and we could see the picture. Chisos Owens was standing before the front door, faced toward Striker and Spanish Jack, who stood by the table. The glass cover of that camphene lamp had been broken, when Elgera had swept it off the table that last time we were here, but it still worked. The light it shed, however, did not reach the other end of the room, and in the shadows over there, with the pale shine of her blonde hair and that strange glow in her blue eyes clearly visible, stood the Scorpion, whip and all.

"You seem to have all the data," said Kelly Striker.

"One word from me will start an investigation that will ruin TSA and you along with it," said Owens.

"And that one word from you would pull Elgera Douglas right down with me," said Striker.

"That's as good as admitting it," said Owens.

Striker shrugged. "Why not? It will never get beyond this house. TSA wiped out most of its resources in the battle to break the Scorpion down here. It would have folded up, if that order for mustangs hadn't come from the Army. But most of the other stock companies had gotten the jump on us and filled all the good sections with their own horse runners. We tried to wangle a deal with the Mexican government, but they wouldn't bite. The only thing left was to run the stuff across the border. It was Jack here who got the idea of picking up the branded stuff. They were already broken, and that would save us the ten dollars a head it cost to have the wild ones busted."

Owens's face was pale and set. There was a little, ragged hole in the leg of his Levi's, high on the right thigh, and the faded cloth bore a dirty bloodstain there. That must have been where the gal's blue whistler caught him when he was skylighted in the door. Not too bad a wound, if he could stand on it like this so soon.

"What makes you think it won't get beyond this house?" he asked Striker.

Striker laughed confidently. "Elgera," he said.

Owens turned to the girl with a sick look on his face. "Tell me, Elgera, tell me just once. That's all I ask. I'll believe you. Anything you say."

"Tell you what?" asked Striker. "Are you still trying to convince yourself that she didn't murder Senator Bailes? Anything you say outside will just make it worse for her."

"He won't have to say *anything*, Kelly," I said, stepping in. "I heard it all."

Striker whirled toward me, surprised as a dogie the first time it's thrown, and all the angles must have passed through his mind in that moment. "Jack!" he shouted.

Jack had wheeled around, too, and had recovered from his surprise enough for his hands to make that fluttering movement. I hauled on my own dewey. The tips of his guns were just clearing the holsters when my first shot caught him. He grunted, and took a step forward, elbows twitching with the effort to lift the guns up. I let another one go at the middle of him, and was twisting for Striker.

He was no gunny, and he had just fought his iron out. I emptied my dewey into him. When his gun exploded, it was pointed the other way, because my shots had spun him around. He fell across Spanish Jack's body on the floor.

Then I saw someone coming at me from the other side of the room, and wheeled that way to see Chisos Owens. His lips were drawn back against his teeth, and his eyes held that gun-metal shine.

"That four-shot house gun don't quite go around, does it?" he said. "I'm sorry it's empty now. You aren't taking Elgera, Marshal. I told you that last time . . . no matter what she did . . . you're not taking her."

I guess he didn't know about my broken arm. Or maybe he would have done it anyway, feeling as he did about the girl.

"Chisos," I said, "don't. It won't be clean. I'm through fighting you clean. I'm taking that girl, and I don't care how I have to do it."

"No, you aren't," he said, going for his gun.

"Well, hell," I told him, and jumped in.

I had that empty Cloverleaf still in my good hand when I reached him, and I brought it down on his gun wrist with all my force. He howled in pain, and the Bisley went spinning out of his hand. He made a swipe at me with his other paw. It caught me on the side of the head as I jumped back. Ears ringing, I tore free and with that hand still held out toward me hit him across that wrist, too, with my dewey. He grunted hoarsely, pulling the hand back instinctively. It gave me an opening, and I wheeled in on that side, lashing him across the side of the face with the gun. It laid his cheek open. Blood spurting, he lurched toward me, trying to get a hold.

I dodged his arms again, and came in on the other flank. He whirled at me, but I caught him again, and jumped away. That one put a stripe across his forehead. Shaking his head dazedly, he came on at me.

I took another shift that put me on the outside with him up

against the wall. I slashed him on one side, and then the other. I tried to get away, but each time he turned one way or the other. I kept driving him back with a blow, but finally he got too close and caught my broken arm. The pain blotted out my sight for a minute. We were in against each other, and the smell of his blood almost gagged me. I slashed blindly at his head, felt him sag downward. He tried to catch my next blow with his free hand, but I changed directions and got past his block. He sagged again beneath the blow.

Yet he wouldn't let go of that broken arm, and I guess I was crying like a baby with the agony of it now. I hit him again, and he slid farther down the wall. His face was up against my belly, but he still wouldn't let go of my arm. Bawling like a stampeded heifer, I still tried to tear loose, and lifted that Cloverleaf for another blow.

"If you hit him again, Marshal," said the Scorpion from behind me somewhere, "I swear, I'll kill you."

I stood there a minute, without turning around. Owens drew in a breath full of broken, hoarse pain. Then his grip on my arm relaxed, and he slid the rest of the way down the wall to sprawl at my feet. It came to me, then, that the Scorpion was still standing at the far end of the room by the fireplace, and there was no gun in her hand. I thought for a moment I'd been tricked. But the voice had come from *behind* me. Something made me turn that way.

The Scorpion, standing in the doorway, held that big Army Colt in her hand. But there was no whip dangling from her left wrist.

"Well," I said, "I should've figured this heifer for twins."

X

Branding a cow was the smartest thing ever done with the critters. I wished, somehow, that somebody had branded those two gals, so we could cut them out and chouse them to their right outfits. But then the brands would probably have been the same, anyway. Everything else was. They both had that hair, pale as a palomino's mane, and those blue eyes with the peculiar glow, and the suede *chivarras* with red roses down the seams. The curves on the one by the fireplace were more obvious and would probably have drawn a man's eye on the street quicker. But a little extra side-bacon doesn't always make a prize hog.

Avarillo had pulled his stingy gun when we first burst into the room, and that was apparently what had held the one over by the fireplace from any movement. But now he tucked it away with a strange, secretive chuckle, which gave the one in the doorway the drop on us.

"I shall relinquish my services now, Marshal." He grinned. "The problem which has presented itself is entirely yours."

"Pick up Chisos," said the one in the doorway, waving her gun.

I helped him onto a chair, where he sat with his head on his arms, making soft, retching sounds. I never knew a man to take such a beating and remain conscious. Spanish Jack was dead, but my two last shots had only caught Striker in the side, spinning him around. Avarillo helped me drag him over against the wall and sit him up, and the Mexican started to build a fire and heat some water for his wounds. Hagar was behind the woman with the Colt, and he moved around her, staring at the other one in a vague, puzzled way.

"Which one is the Scorpion, Hagar?" I asked.

He jerked his narrow head at the one with the Colt. "This one, of course."

"Are you sure?" said the one by the fireplace in that husky voice. "Are you sure, Johnny?"

He started to speak angrily, then checked himself. The one by the fireplace laughed throatily.

"The way I got it figured," I said, "Striker didn't take everyone on the board of directors of TSA into his confidence when he started running these Mexican mustangs across. Bailes was one of those on the board who wouldn't have accepted it. But he was also in a position to uncover it, if anything aroused his suspicions. And that's just what he had done when he sent that wire from Alpine to Washington, assuring them that he had evidence that would stop the mustang running. Striker had to stop him or be ruined. Striker had been trying to break the Scorpion down here for a long time, and this gave him a chance to kill two birds. He imported a gal from somewhere who was the Scorpion's double. He had her ride into town and kill Bailes, which naturally put the genuine Scorpion out among the willows."

"That's very clever," said Avarillo, "but, if Hagar, who has known her for years and who has been in love with her, cannot tell, in the final analysis, which one is the real Scorpion, how are you going to decide?"

"Let's all go outside . . . except for Chisos," I said.

The one with the Colt finally agreed. Owens's dun with the arched mane and Hagar's apron-faced horse were out there, along with Spanish Jack's black and Striker's animal. And two palomino mares. One was hitched to a support of the porch roof. I unhitched her and led her away from the house in case of a ruckus. Then I put my foot in the ox-yoke and swung aboard. She was a spirited beast, and started side-stepping and cavorting, but I didn't have too much trouble handling her. I dismounted and ground-hitched her. Then I went over toward the mare hooked to a cottonwood some yards from the house. This one started snorting and hauling at its bridle before I was within ten feet. The nostrils fluttered, and the eyes rolled at me like shiny glass. The muscles began to ripple and twitch beneath its fine, pale skin.

"All right," I told the girl who had stood by the fireplace. "You step in this tree."

Her lips pinched in for a minute. Then she shrugged and walked toward the horse. The animal jumped around the same as it had before, fuming and whinnying. It allowed the gal to unhook it, though, and throw the reins over its head. But when she lifted her foot to the stirrup, the mare spun away.

With a curse like a man, she hauled on the reins. The spade bit in the critter's mouth caused it to wheel back fast with that vicious jerk on the reins. The girl jumped on its back without using stirrups. She hadn't found them when the buttermilk horse started chinning the moon. It cat-backed and double-shuffled and then went into a high binder that looked fit to split a cloud. Coming out of that, it sunfished with such a violent wrench the girl lost her seat and spilled out of the yannigan bag. The horse galloped off a few hundred feet, wheeling around down there in nervous circles, snorting and squealing.

"How about you?" I told the one with the Colt.

She looked at me, then started walking toward the horse. We watched without saying anything. The girl on the ground sat up, shaking her head dazedly. The other one reached the horse and looked like she was talking to it. Then she stepped on and brought the mare back to us in the prettiest little Spanish walk I ever saw.

I moved over to the gal on the ground. "You're under arrest," I said, "for the murder of Senator Warren Bailes."

Rae Stewart was her name. She told us the whole story. She had been a rodeo queen. I figured it would take some kind of tough one like that to go through with Striker's plan—she had been in love with Striker in Waco, and he had enough influence over her to rope her in on this roundup. She and Striker had been using this house as a rendezvous after Elgera Douglas had been forced into the tulles by the law. Rae was the one who had shot Chisos Owens here at the Santiago that time. It was the real Scorpion who had picked me up out on the Comanche Trail and had taken me to Avarillo's, and who had saved me from getting my lights put out by Bryce Wylie. She had been trailing the herd of mustangs Wylie was driving at that time. Instead of driving them herself, she had been waiting till they got up around Alpine, so she could stampede them again the way she had that other herd, in the hopes of breaking up the rustling and exposing Striker's connection.

We all had some much needed shut-eye at the Santiago, and a good breakfast the next morning. Striker's wounds weren't so bad that he couldn't stand the ride north. I took the horses down to the creek for water just before we left, and Elgera said she'd show me the good places.

"That was clever about La Rubia," she said.

"That means The Blonde, doesn't it?" I said. "I'd heard you were the only one who could fork that buttermilk horse of yours."

"Si Samson sent one of his stable boys down to the Rosillos with news that Chisos was dying here," she said. "You did that on purpose?"

"That grapevine you've got should make Morse blush for shame," I told her. "I figured you'd fog in, if you heard the man you loved was sacking his saddle."

"He's just a very good friend," she said.

"Hagar, too, I suppose," I said.

She nodded, pouting a little.

"How about that time down in the Dead Horses with Wylie?" I asked.

"Don't thank me," she said.

"I'm not talking about how you saved my life," I said. "You know what I'm talking about."

"All right," she answered. "How about it?"

"Was it ever like that . . . with Chisos . . . or Hagar?" I asked.

She started to answer, then closed her mouth. The pout grew.

"I guess not," I said, and did what I'd been talking about again.

When I stopped kissing her, the lids of her eyes were dropped heavily, like a sleepy kid's, and she was staring at me with the same expression on her face I'd seen down in the Dead Horses that time.

"I've got a little duty to do," I told her. "But I'll be back."

"I'm not making any promises, Powder," she said.

"I am," I told her. "I'll be back."

"Snuffy little bronc'," she said, "aren't you?"

★ ★ ★ ★ ★

BUCKSKIN BORDER

★ ★ ★ ★ ★

Les Savage, Jr., finished this short novel in early May, 1947 and sent it to his agent, August Lenniger. It was sent at once to K. Rafferty, the editor of Dell Publishing's *Five-Novels Magazine,* who accepted it on May 15, 1947. The original title was "Buckskin Border" and it was published under this title in the issue dated November-December, 1947. The author was paid $450.00. It was Savage's first and, as it turned out, only story published in this magazine. *Five-Novels Magazine* ceased publication with the January-February, 1948 issue, bringing to a close its twenty-year publication history.

I

The time was 1844, the place the Upper Missouri near the headwaters in what is now North Dakota and Montana. All along the border tempers were flaming. It looked as if war between Great Britain and the States might break out at any moment. Root of the dispute was this territory, jointly occupied by Britain and the United States. The States claimed everything up to the fifty-fourth parallel; the slogan "Fifty-Four Forty or Fight" had swept the country during Polk's campaign the year before. But the British refused to grant any territory north of the forty-ninth parallel.

Furs were getting scarcer now, and this was valuable fur country. Rival British and American fur-trapping companies would stop at little to protect their charters and their trap routes. The Indians, too, were at the breaking point, for each fur company tried to incite different tribes to attack its rivals.

Shade Cameron could not help the groan that slipped from his pinched lips as he dragged himself up out of the frozen buckbrush. He lay heavily on the snow, blood from his wounded chest spreading beneath his body. There were lines of pain etched about his eyes and mouth.

Then the focus of his eyes lost its blur and he distinguished the figure in the underbrush along the creekbank. The man was hunkered down in the bushes with a rifle across his knees. The two men stared at each other for a measureless time. Finally Shade could stand it no longer.

"Well, shoot, damn you, and get it over with," he gasped, the words coming out hoarsely and thickly.

Still the man did not move. His head was shaven bald, and his eyes were jet beads in the carven Indian face. His buffalo robe hid all but his moccasins. They were decorated with turquoise beads in a fashion Shade had never seen on the Indians of the Upper Missouri before. A faint breeze came down off the slope, rattling through the buckbrush. Then that ceased, and the white world about them was still again.

Shade's trap-scarred fingers dug into the crust of snow, and he lowered his face, trying to find strength for movement. But he was giddy and sick and unable to go farther. The blood soaking his elk-hide leggings had already begun to congeal, freezing them to the snow. He did not know how long he lay there, after that. He might have passed out. In his next lucid moment he heard the voice of the Indian in the bushes.

"They were Hidatsa Indians?"

"I don't know," mumbled Shade. "Would Indians be packing enough rifles to cut me up like this? What's that got to do with it? They might have been American Fur Company for all I know."

"Why should American Fur want you?" asked the man. There was the faint trace of accent in his speech.

"How should I know?" gasped Shade. "Aren't you with them?"

"I heard the shooting upstream," said the Indian. "They might still be around. I'm not going to take the chance of moving from this cover. Can you crawl over to the brush?"

Shade did not waste his remaining strength on words. As volition seeped through his muscles, an overpowering desire to sleep went with it. Each breath he took seemed to cut his lungs and then seep out the bullet holes, fingering the bloody flesh with probing malignancy. His elk hides made a small ripping sound pulling free of the ice. He was not conscious of moving, but finally the brush was *crackling* beneath his body. When he was up to his waist in the bushes, the man reached out a hand to grasp his wrist and pull him in. The fingers were like talons, and, when the Indian had pulled him completely into cover and released his grip, Shade could see the white indentations circling his own bony wrist. *Last time I seen a grip like that was on a Kentucky log runner,* thought Shade, and passed out. . . .

II

The next thing he felt was warmth at his feet. His eyes opened abruptly as the pain returned. He was lying on his back in the fetid stink of buffalo robes, feet toward a *crackling* fire. He realized he must have been carried to this camp, and that it must be some distance from the creek where he had been shot up, to risk an open fire this way.

The Indian who had brought Shade in was standing with his back to Shade. There was another man beyond who looked like a half-breed. He had a vicious black-bearded face beneath a fur cap with earflaps turned up. His bulky red Mackinaw failed to hide a torso so tremendous it looked top-heavy on short bowed legs. Another man squatted in the shadows.

"I say you should have left him there, Akomo," the half-breed was telling the Indian. "They might have followed you."

"I don't think so, Wachee," the Indian murmured. "I stayed there in the brush an hour after he crawled out of the creek before I pulled him in. I'm sure they didn't follow him."

Wachee moved one arm in the red Mackinaw in a violent gesture. "You're taking too much on yourself, dammit, both you and that woman. . . ."

"Don't say anything about her you'd be sorry for, Wachee," said Akomo. He had not raised his voice, but it cut off the other man sharply. They stood staring at each other for a moment.

Wachee's breath made a heavy, harsh sound against the *crackling* of the fire.

Wachee's gaze shifted toward Shade. He moved around the Indian and lowered himself to a squatting position beside Shade. Then he reached down a hairy hand, thick fingers probing Shade's chest mercilessly until Shade winced.

"Up high, probably not a lung," growled the man casually. "So it was American Fur Company men."

"Was it?" said Shade. "I thought American Fur handed this territory over to Hudson's Bay years ago."

"Their men are still around," said Wachee. He began to probe for the leg wound. "What have they got against you?"

"How should I know?" snapped Shade, driven to a raw anger by the man's insistent pointless probing.

"A poacher, maybe," said Wachee.

Perhaps it was the pain, slowing Shade's reactions. "No, I. . . ." He hesitated, searching the man's face for some sign. Wachee jabbed his finger at the wound in Shade's thigh.

"That's right. You're not a poacher. Is that what you were going to say? That's what I thought. Maybe you're American Fur yourself. Or something else. I don't think it was the Company. I think those were Hidatsa Indians trying to kill you. And why should the Indians want you dead so bad? They don't bother Hudson's Bay trappers. What are you doing up here, porkeater?"

Even in his pain, Shade's face turned red at the insult. Porkeaters were the bound laborers who worked inside the forts—the worst insult you could give a trapper. He tried to raise up, but the man's hand held him down, starting that cruel pointless probing again. "I don't think you're a trapper at all. Take him back where you found him and leave him there, Akomo."

"No. Hold him for Ione to see," said Akomo, starting to shift toward the man and raise his rifle.

"Take him back," said Wachee, spinning, still hunkered down so that the Jake Hawkens rifle under one elbow came to bear on the Indian about belly height.

Akomo halted his forward motion with such an abrupt jerk that his buffalo robe slipped off his shoulders and piled up at his feet. His eyes were on that big Hawkens rifle, but it was not that which must have held him. It was the sound the third man had made, rising from where he had been hunkering in the shadow behind Wachee. He wore the white blanket coat of a French-Canadian *voyageur.*

"Akomo doesn't want to do what I tell him, Vide," Wachee told the white-coated *voyageur.* "Maybe you'd better take our poacher back. Leave him in a nice open spot. The wolves are pretty hungry about this time of year."

"*Mais oui,* Wachee," said Vide, and started to step around the fire.

"*Mais non,* Vide," said a clear voice from the edge of the timber. "If you take another step, it won't be the Yankee who feeds those wolves."

By then Shade had twisted enough to see the slim tall figure standing by the naked trees, with the pistol in her hand.

I'd like me a jug of sugar-top whiskey, he thought dimly. I'd like me a jug of sugar-top to throw over my shoulder and empty at one gulp and make me burn so from head to toe I couldn't even feel this pain in my chest. Maybe it was that pain which kept him from hearing exactly what they were saying over there.

The woman had come on in from the trees, with that pistol still in evidence. The shaggy brown buffalo coat she wore obscured the lines of her figure above the hips, but her legs were long and slender in a pair of leggings fringed with what looked suspiciously like black human hair. Her voice sounded angry, and she kept making violent little jerks with the pistol.

Wachee's answers became shorter and shorter, and finally he shrugged.

The woman turned and came over to Shade.

"You haven't even taken care of him," she said sharply, crouching down beside the trapper, and tucked the pistol away beneath her coat, starting to give orders. "Pull his feet away from that fire. Can't you see they're frozen? Take his moccasins off, Akomo. Get some snow to rub on them, Vide. Oh, you fools, look at him. We'll be lucky if he doesn't die anyway. Get some oak bark off the slope, if you can find it. Dig in my possible sack for that Indian meal we got off the Mandans. We'll thicken it with charcoal and boil it to make a poultice for these wounds. It's the best we can do till we get to Fort Bliss. . . ."

She had begun to open Shade's shirt, but stopped as she saw his eyes on her. They were so slitted with pain she must have thought they were closed at first. A momentary uncertainty crossed her face. Her reaction was so completely feminine it almost made him laugh. She reached self-consciously up toward the hat as if to see whether her hair were in place.

"Horse sort of switched ends quick," he muttered.

Her lips were surprisingly full for the narrow aristocracy of her face, and their smile revealed even white teeth. "I'm sorry about Wachee." She shrugged, peeling at his shirt. "Things are sort of touchy up this way now."

"You're Hudson's Bay fur trappers?" he said.

She shook her head. "Ojibway Fur."

"The company that pulled away from the Bay," said Shade. "That sort of puts you in between things, doesn't it?"

"Most of our men are still British."

"Why should Wachee be so het up whether it was Hidatsa Indians or American Fur Company trappers that shot me up?" he said.

"When the Company pulled out, a lot of their men remained,"

she said. "They call themselves free trappers, but they still run in their old brigades. They're really nothing more than white renegades." Her lips lost that richness, pinching to a thin line. "It was American Fur Company men who perpetrated the Fort Bliss massacre, in which my father was killed." She sat in that way a moment longer, then tossed her head, as if returning from something by a defiant effort. "I guess I should introduce myself. Ione Napier."

"Shade Cameron," he told her.

"Kentucky?"

"You got an eye," he said.

"The way you talk, maybe," she said, her eyes dropping to his hands. "You haven't got enough trap scars there to be a full-time trapper. What's your business up here?"

"Nothing, professionally," he said. "Running the woods mostly. I'm a restless man."

"A woods runner," she said. There was a speculative light to her eyes. "You're out of your time. That went out with Daniel Boone, didn't it?"

"I guess I was born a little late," he said. "Most men come West to trap or find new land for themselves or trade. I just came to see the country."

"You look like a runner," she said, glancing at the taut line of his long legs. "A deer. Like Akomo, in a way."

"Tarahumare from Mexico, isn't he?" asked Shade.

She glanced sharply at him. "How would you know that?"

"A traveling man sees a bit of country," he said. "I was in the Mexican Sierras about four years back. They say some of those Indians can outrun a horse. I never saw one speak English, though."

"Akomo came North young." She had finished bandaging him up with that stinging poultice, and now had Vide lift him up to wrap a buffalo robe about his body. He felt warm and drowsy, the pain growing dull. She gave him a last glance, then rose, turning toward the fire.

Wachee and Vide drifted from his sight. He did not know how Akomo had gotten there. Maybe walked over from the fire. The man's bronzed saturnine face swam into his sight abruptly.

"A woods runner," said Akomo.

"Yeah," said Shade. "We'll have to race sometime."

"You would not want that," said Akomo.

"Why not?" said Shade.

"Because where I come from," answered the man, his voice hissing with that sibilance, as soft as a whisper yet not actually a whisper, "when two men race, they run till one of them drops dead, and that is the way it would have to be with you and me, one way, or another."

III

They brought the pony into camp four days after Shade arrived. It was a moon-eyed little broomtail, shaggy with its black coat of winter hair. They might have gotten it from one of the Mandan Indian camps farther down the river.

The pony was pulling an Indian travois, the kind usually used for transporting bundles. It consisted of two birch-wood poles lashed together to make a V, with the point at the top, resting on the horse's withers, the two ends dragging.

They lashed Shade into the sling between the smoked birch poles. Then the men slipped into the straps of their packing cases. Ione went over and carefully obliterated the fire by kicking snow across the pile of ashes. Vide took the pony's rope hackamore in his hand and turned his back on the animal. Shade stiffened to the first small pain the jolt of starting caused him.

Where the Cannonball River ran into the Missouri, Shade noticed their surprised perturbation. Wachee had left camp early that morning to scout ahead before they moved, and he came back scratching his beard. The woman rose from the fire and crossed to him. Shade could overhear only part of what they said.

"Hidatsa?" said Ione.

"Don't be a fool," growled Wachee. "No Hidatsa's going to wear shoes like that. Looks more like a Cree shoe. I know the pattern."

"What would a Cree be doing this far south?"

"Nothing," he said. "But a Hudson's Bay man might."

After that, Shade began working at one of the whangs on the fringe of his elk hides. He freed three of the crimson-dyed elk-hide strips from the fringe and held them in his hand till the party moved out of camp onto the trail. Then he let them slip into the snow.

At the confluence of the Little Heart and the Missouri, Wachee must have found more sign. Tension mounted in camp, and Wachee kept Vide out all night scouting the surrounding country.

That morning, as they began march again, Shade let another trio of crimson whangs drop from his hand into the snow. There was something hunted in Wachee's keen little eyes now, a constant puzzlement, and he kept leaving the line of march. He'd be gone an hour or more, returning with the puzzlement intensified.

"If I thought it was Hidatsa or Blackfeet, I wouldn't care," Shade overheard him telling Ione that evening at supper. "But this is crazy. What do they want? Why don't they come in?"

That night, with the moon spilling its pale winter light into the sleeping camp, Shade awoke from a fitful sleep to the mournful *hoot* of an owl. He lay there, trying to figure out what it was about the owl hoot that was wrong. Then he realized what it was. The sound kept shifting back and forth.

He saw that Vide had stiffened in his blankets where he was on watch. In another moment Wachee rolled from his robes with a muffled curse, reaching for his Mackinaw and long Jake Hawkens rifle. This must have awakened Ione.

"What is it?" she said.

"I don't know," snarled Wachee. "I'm tired of playing hide-and-seek, that's all. That ain't no owl. The Crees used to make war signals that way up by the Peace. I'm going out to see who's out there."

Ione rose, pulling her big pistol to check the priming. "I'm going with you."

"I don't care," said Wachee. "Leave your Indian here for Kentucky. Come on, Empty Pockets."

Vide Poche (in English his name meant Empty Pocket) climbed out of his blankets and followed Wachee across the clearing to black timber, Ione taking up the rear.

Only then was Shade aware of Akomo. The Indian must have been first to awake, and had stood there in plain view all the time, so quiet and relaxed that even Shade had missed him till now. It filled the Kentuckian with an uncanny chill. But he saw how the man's wooden face was turned after the three who were disappearing into the trees.

"Don't you think she can take care of herself?" he said.

Akomo's face turned toward him sharply. The movement itself was the only indication Shade had of the man's feelings, for the Indian's face bore no expression. Then, with a swift decision, he moved over and hunkered down beside Shade, moving the buffalo robe off his wounded leg.

"That's right," said Shade. "I can't go far on that. Maybe you better go after her."

Moonlight made black glitter in Akomo's eyes. With an audible exhalation, he rose and slipped off toward the trees.

When he had disappeared, Shade threw the robe completely off and crawled to the Green River knife stuck in a log by the fire; it was the only weapon in evidence. He tried to rise, but his leg would not support him. He crawled toward the timber on the opposite side of the clearing from the direction Wachee and the others had taken. He crawled through the barren poplars till he reached a gully obscured by bare chokecherry branches. He halted here and *hooted* like an owl. He did this twice more before he was answered softly.

In a moment, there was the dim *splush* of passage through snowdrift. A man appeared abruptly, in black silhouette, and stood there on the lip of the depression.

"They thought there must be fifty-four Crees out here giving owl hoots," said Shade.

"Only forty," said the man.

"Either that or fight," Shade murmured.

The man slid down the slush to come on his hunkers beside Shade. He had a rifle tucked under one arm; its ironwork showed some use, but still held a new gleam to its sheen. He was lean and whip-like within the square drape of his red coat made from a Hudson's Bay four-point blanket. His eyes were cold and detached, and his bloodless lips seemed to form the words without movement.

"I'm Benedict, with the United States government," said the man.

"I'm Cameron," Shade told him. "Government agent. They thought you were lost up here. That's why they sent me out. What happened?"

"My contact man was at Fort Rice, up near Long Lake," said Benedict. "When Rice was wiped out last December, I didn't have any way to send word in. He identified himself to me by the same red whangs, torn from the fringe of his buckskins. When I spotted them on this trail, I figured I'd take the chance on a new one being sent out."

"They said you'd give some kind of Cree sign, if you were still alive," Shade told him. "When Wachee spotted those Cree shoe tracks, I thought maybe you'd come in on those red whangs."

"How long you been with them?" asked Benedict.

"I been in this country since November, feeling around, trying to get a line on something," said Shade. "Somebody began tailing me a couple of weeks back. Bunch of Hidatsa jumped me at Patchskin Buttes."

"The Indians are on everybody's neck, with this border trouble going on," said Benedict.

"I shot a couple of them, and then I got away by diving through the ice and floating downstream underneath," said Shade. "Akomo picked me up. He showed too much interest in who shot me, so I let him draw his own conclusions. He figured the Hidatsa being such poor shots, they wouldn't have enough guns to shoot me up like that. Wachee was only half convinced American Fur men did it."

"Good," said Benedict. "With their British connections, you'll be right in their own possible sack if they think American Fur Company men shot you up. They won't even care if you were poaching on American lines. They consider them poachers to begin with. And if they have more than just British connections. . . ."

"Couple of suspicious things," said Shade. "They weren't setting out any trap lines."

"That's what made me trail them, before I found your whangs," said Benedict. "I came across their sign a few days ago. Took them for a party of trappers. But I didn't find any traps. That got me suspicious. That's why I decided to take a look."

"What would they be doing down this way?" said Shade.

Benedict studied that. "Fort Renville's a little to the west."

"Think it might be next?" said Shade.

Benedict shrugged. "Who knows? Does Washington still think the British are behind this border trouble?"

"An H.B.C. commission was found on one of the dead bodies at the Fort Rice massacre," said Shade.

Benedict snorted in disgust. "Hudson's Bay Company has a motive, of course. As long as they can keep the treaty from being settled, and this remains joint occupancy territory, they're sure of trapping charters here. But that doesn't prove anything. The Crown has good cause for believing Americans are behind the trouble, too. Two men known to be closely connected with Astor, head of American Fur, were found among the dead at the Fort Bliss massacre." Benedict leaned forward, pinning Shade with those chill eyes. "The trouble has long ago taken on a pattern that points to an organization. But I don't think it's either H.B.C. or what's left of Astor's company. It's someone else, deliberately interested in bringing about a war. That 'Fifty-Four Forty or Fight' slogan is on everybody's lips. Another massacre like the Fort Rice affair and the United States will declare war on Britain for sure." He bent farther forward. "Do you think this is a lead?"

"It's the first opening we've had," said Shade.

The man looked at his wounds. "You're in a helluva state to follow it up."

"That's why you'd better stick around . . . on the outside," said Shade. "They seem to be taking me to Fort Bliss. I'll see what information I can get. We can keep in touch, but whatever you do, don't show unless I yell for help. If I'm on the inside, I want that card up my sleeve."

"Fort Bliss," murmured Benedict. "They say Christian York's taken it over since Paul Napier was killed."

"Anything on him?"

"York was in the British Intelligence during the War of Eighteen Twelve," said Benedict. "Dishonorably discharged, but that might be a camouflage for his present activities. I know the Crown has several agents on this thing, too."

"Do they have any password to identify each other?"

"It's similar to ours, I've heard," said Benedict. "They add or subtract or something till they come out with the Fifty-Four Forty slogan. I don't know that they'd work with us if we did find them now, though. I. . . ."

"Above you!" yelled Shade, trying to grab Benedict and pull him aside from the figure appearing so suddenly on the lip of the gully. And then a small avalanche of snow struck them with the man leaping down and a guttural shout in the semidarkness deafened Shade. Even with the snow blinding him, he had the dim sense of a twisted face and a vicious club raised above Benedict's head.

He went on with his sweeping motion to throw Benedict aside, and threw himself beside the agent, in beneath the club. He knocked the other man back against the slush, the blow striking his own back with an aborted sound.

"Get out!" he shouted to Benedict, the words issuing in a gasp with the force of that blow.

Then, writhing to twist over on the assailant and get beneath him, he felt the hard bulk of the body stiffen and knew it was for another blow. He rolled aside, catching the club as it went down, and allowed his body to go on over into the snow, its inertia providing weight enough to wrench the club free. His palms were cut by the sharp edge. He came to his knees, shifting his grip.

Again it was that sense of twisted face and oncoming silhouette, as the man leaped at him. Still on his knees, he swung back the club. The jumping figure hurtled right into the blow. Shade had never heard such utter sick agony in any cry.

The man's body struck him and rode him down. His own body was filled with gathered tension to roll free, when he felt how limp and dead the weight of the man against him was. He relaxed tentatively, then squirmed from beneath. His old leg wound must have been opened, for his elk hides were damp with blood again. Each labored panting breath seemed to draw the air like the blade of a knife through the bullet hole in his chest. He was dizzy and nauseated and had trouble focusing his eyes.

Benedict was nowhere in sight. That pleased Shade in a thin ironic way. The man might not make a good friend, but he was a good agent. Then Shade stared at the weapon in his hand. It was about three feet long and shaped like a mace, the heavy dense wood forming a knob at its end, and the obsidian attached to its edges beneath the knob giving it the lethal, dual function of a club and sword.

"A Mexican Indian *guayacán*," he murmured, raising his eyes to the man lying face down in the snow. "I sort of figured it might be you, Akomo."

IV

Christian York said: "Of course, you were quite right in bringing Mister Cameron to Fort Bliss as soon as he was well enough to travel."

Not many men Christian York's size could have minced. He moved his oleaginous bulk through the room with dainty, almost feminine posturing. He never looked directly at Shade. His face turned now toward the undressed pine logs of the ceiling, or toward the grizzly pelts on the wall, his plump wet lips forming a swinish profile beneath the red bulb of his nose.

He reached the fireplace and turned there, placing his hands behind his ample posterior and spreading his legs and thrusting his great belly forward.

"And Akomo, I can't understand that. He isn't the type, somehow, to just"—he made a fatuous gesture with one doughy hand—"disappear. You say Cameron was the only one in camp when you returned?"

"Yes," said Ione. "There must have been a dozen trails made by that Cree around camp, and by the time Wachee and Vide and I had separated and finally found all the trails were made by the same pair of snowshoes, we'd spent several hours at it. When we got back, Shade told us Akomo had gone out after the same Cree. When he hadn't returned next morning, we trailed him to a gully. There was a snowbank caved in, and two trails leading away northward, one made by these same Cree shoes, the other by Akomo's moccasins. We lost both of them within a mile or so."

As she spoke, Shade watched her face. He could find no sign of guile. She seemed quite convinced of the little story he had left for them, with those tracks. He had buried Akomo deep in that snowbank. Then, to take their attention off of it, if they searched, he had donned the Tarahumare's moccasins himself. Managing to stay erect long enough, with the aid of trees and brush and drifts, he had made a trail following Benedict's for a few hundred yards. Finally, reaching a thick portion of buck-brush, where he could make his way back to camp, he had discarded the moccasins in a tree and crawled in, obliterating the sign he made from there on. He wished he could have slipped back to the drift to make sure Akomo was really dead, but he never got a chance. He must be, though, or he'd have come in.

"Why," said Christian York, "should American Fur want to shoot you up like that, Cameron?"

"What makes you think it was American Fur?" said Shade.

"Oh, come now," said York petulantly. "Why not admit it, Cameron? Wachee told me. Were you poaching on their trap lines? We don't care really, you know. In fact, we are inclined to sympathize with you. If it was, I don't suppose you'll be left with much love for them."

"I never had much love anyhow."

"Oh well, now." York chuckled. "That's interesting."

York allowed his gaze to cross Ione's for a moment, and she rose. "You'll excuse me?"

"Of course, my dear." The fat man chuckled. He accompanied Ione to the door.

Then she was gone, and York closed the door. "And now, Cameron," he said, "I understand you Kentuckians are famous as imbibers of spirits. Perhaps it would not be out of line to offer you some of ours. Unfortunately not up to what you could get nearer civilization. We have to supply ourselves. I hope it will suffice."

"Funny to find a girl traveling with a trapping party," said Shade.

York hesitated a moment, then went on turning the bung starter of the cask on a table. "Ione is an unusual girl, Cameron. Match a man on the trail, spot a prime pelt quicker than most I know."

"Wachee," said Shade absently. "Up by Athabaska in Canada that means hello in Cree."

York nodded in a pleased way. "You have seen country, haven't you? Yes, Wachee got his name in the Territories. They say it's a corruption of the greeting the Englishmen used to use. 'What cheer' . . . or something like that. Could be. The Indians pick up a lot of words like that." He handed one of the glasses to Shade. "Traveling so much, you must see a lot, Cameron."

"Like what?" asked Shade.

York shrugged. "You know all the trouble going on up here, of course. Getting so a man can't ply a decent fur trade without having to battle every renegade south of the Canadian Territories as well as both governments. Even right in the middle of it, though, we don't see everything that's going on. These trappers who shot you up. Why should they do that? Poaching? That's the natural conclusion Wachee reached." He had paced to the other end of the room, and turned toward Shade. "But you don't strike me as that stripe, somehow? What was it, Cameron? They're a bunch of renegades, you know. Had you discovered their post?"

"Post?" said Shade.

The first impatience clawed at York's face as he straightened from peering at Shade. "What an eternal reticence, Mister Cameron. Yes, post . . . post, their fort, where they operate from."

"They been causing you trouble?" said Shade.

"Who do you think perpetrated the massacre in this very fort, when Paul Napier was killed?" asked York. Then he saw the pained expression twisting Shade's mouth and jerked a fat hand in petulant impatience. "I won't apologize for the drink. It's nothing but Indian grog, but it's the best we can manage up here."

"What kind of corn you make it from?" asked the Kentuckian.

"The Mandans call it maize."

"I don't see no reason why you couldn't get some good old Kentucky sugar-top whiskey out of this," said Shade.

York's interest was piqued. "Believe me, Cameron, I'd be eternally grateful to the man who got some decent spirits in this wilderness. I haven't had anything worth calling whiskey since I was in York Factory on the Bay, and that was four years ago."

"Where do you keep your mash barrels?"

"In the loft usually," said York.

"No wonder you don't get anything better than this hogwash," Shade said. "Whenever it gets cold enough up there, the mash stops fermenting. Fifty pounds of sugar to the bushel of cornmeal and sprouts, and bury it in the ground in a bed of straw. That's the only way to get decent Kentucky mash out of it."

"How about working on that?" said York.

"Like some myself," said Shade. "I'll need a few things."

York walked to the door, opened it to the outer room of the building. Cameron watched him out of narrowed eyes, waiting.

"Delede," York called out, "give Cameron here whatever he needs and mark it up to the company!"

Cameron rose from the chair, turning to go. He had to wait for York to move from the doorway. The ponderous factor stood there a moment, that sly grin on his fat lips. "Yes." He chuckled. "I always manage to see that everyone gets what he deserves, Cameron. It is something you should keep in mind with a man like me."

His chuckle followed Shade out into the larger room, and then the door shut with a *click*. After that, the only sound was the *snapping* of the fire. There was a group hunkered around the fireplace at the other end of the room. Wachee rose from there.

"So you and the *bourgeois*, the boss, had a little talk," he said.

"That's right," said Shade, and moved toward the counter. He was still stiff from those wounds and limped a bit on his bad leg. "You got any kind of piping, Delede?" Shade asked the clerk.

Delede was a tall lean youth, his Indian blood apparent in the straight black hair and unreadable eyes, but his complexion was white. "York ordered some lead pipe for plumbing but it hasn't come yet."

"Give me half a dozen of those rifle barrels, then," said Shade.

"Hear that, Empty Pockets." Wachee grinned. "What do you suppose he could use them for?"

Vide Poche was coming over from the group now. "No telling, Wachee. Maybe he's going shooting, *hein?*"

99

The little Frenchman pulled at the leather-wrapped hilt of a knife thrust in his boot, and began flipping the weapon into the air. Wachee bellied up to the counter beside Shade, putting his elbows on the planks and shifting his weight forward against them.

"Are you going shooting, Cameron," said Wachee.

"This is for worms," said Shade casually. "A Jake Hawkens rifle barrel has plenty of whip. It should be soft enough to fill with sand and bend around a post to make a spiral. Then we'll have to joint the rifle barrels together somehow."

Vide moved in on the other side of Shade, flipping the knife again. "That sounds like whiskey makings."

"Best sugar-top you ever oiled your gullet with," said Shade. "A couple of them empty tarred barrels, too, Delede."

Delede gave Wachee a strange look as he laid the gun barrels on the counter, and Wachee let out a harsh laugh, slapping Shade on the back. "Well, that's fine, Cameron. Did you hear him, Vide? Already he's making himself useful to the boss. I guess Christian really appreciates that. He's wanted some good liquor up here so long."

"*Oui.*" Vide laughed, slapping Shade on the back. "I guess it makes things easier than if Christian didn't think he was useful here."

Shade could not help flinching with the pain that second slap sent through him. He stifled an impulse to whirl toward Vide, realizing that was exactly what they wanted. Instead, he drew a thin breath, speaking carefully to Delede, as the half-breed rolled the second barrel out.

"I'll need a knife, too. One with plenty of weight in the haft."

"*Oui,* and what are you going to do with that?" wondered Vide, flipping his knife again.

"I guess I'll use it to shave the corn sprouts," said Shade, hefting the knife Delede had laid out, and then wheeled casually to one side and heaved it. "And anything else that might come up."

The knife made a *thump* against the wall at the extreme end of the room. None of them must have realized fully what had happened in that first moment following his throw, for the expressions did not enter Vide's face or Wachee's until after the Green River knife had stopped quivering in the undressed pine log. There had been an Indian ceremonial rattle attached by a rawhide thong to a peg in the wall. The rattle now lay on the floor, its thong severed by the knife buried an inch deep in the wall.

"*Sacre nom,*" mumbled Vide Poche, his eyes widening in a surprise that was almost ludicrous, "*sacre nom du bon Dieu.*" A nervous giggle escaped him, as he bent over to slip his own knife back into his boot. "Let us hope nothing else does come up, *m'sieu,* and that you never do have any occasion to use it for more than shaving your corn sprouts."

V

Ice on the creek was breaking up, but the willows were still bare where Shade had erected his still. Some of the *engagés,* the laborers and clerks inside the fort, had helped him build a rock furnace and put the tank in it. It was here Ione found him one day, several weeks after they had arrived. She came from the stockade through snow that still patched the ground. There was a swing to her walk and with it her plaid wool skirt swirled against bare calves. Shade stopped work on the still to watch.

"I brought you some lunch," she said. "Seems you're spending more and more time down here."

He looked at the tin plate of food when she drew the napkin off, and a slow flush crept into his face as he raised his glance to hers. "Why you always trying to prod me?"

She stiffened. "What do you mean?"

"I may sleep inside the walls, but I ain't no pork-eater."

She looked down at the greasy pork in the plate, and something like surprise flashed through her eyes. "Shade, I had no idea. . . ."

"I think you did have an idea," he said.

Her eyes flashed up to his, and the angry toss of her head sent glints of light bobbing over blue-black curls. "You're being stupid. That's a childish attitude of the trappers anyway, not wanting pork just because the *engagés* eat it."

"There's nothing childish about not wanting to be identified with a bunch of whining varmints more woman than man, that sleep inside the walls three hundred and sixty-five days out of the year and wouldn't touch their lily-white hands to a trap for fear it'd bite 'em, and get fat as canebrake hogs on lard like this," he said.

She laughed suddenly, and it took him off balance. He turned toward the still uncomfortably, seeing if there weren't something about the spiral worm for distilling that he could adjust. "What's funny?" he muttered.

"Nothing, really." She smiled. "It's just so typical of you. Not wanting to be soft. In any way. Hard as iron on a Hawkens rifle and tough as the whangs on your elk hides and gritty as the smell of powder, and fighting at every turn to stay that way. Is that why you won't accept me, Shade?"

"A man gets jumpy around a woman when he's spent most of his life running the woods alone, I guess," said Shade. "We do seem to be looking at each other down a gun barrel every time we meet, don't we? I will take the corndodgers, though."

"They're pemmican cakes," she said.

He shrugged, sitting on a rock to munch one. "Fort Bliss belonged to your father before York became the factor. How did you escape them American Fur Company trappers when they killed your dad?"

Her face darkened. "I was out on a trap line. When I came back, the fort was burning and there was no one inside but the dead. York had known Father, and, when he started extending Ojibway Fur down this way, he rebuilt Fort Bliss with my consent. He gave me a contract for a percentage of the net on the pelts within the region my father had formerly controlled."

"I don't blame you for hostility to American Fur, but why extend it to every Yankee trapper?"

Her voice grew heated. "Because they're all in that same category more or less, lawless, godless, ungoverned savages, running in bunches or alone, it doesn't matter, causing all this trouble up here. You won't find Hudson's Bay brigades or Ojibway Fur men raiding and looting and plundering like that. Even Astor, bad as he was, wouldn't have allowed it. But now that he's retired, they're no better than. . . ."

"That's what I mean," he said, watching the bitterness on her face. "If you feel so strongly about it, why should you make an exception of me?"

It brought her up short. She studied him, her rapid breathing subsiding. He took a last bite of the pemmican cake, then he wiped his greasy fingers on his elk hides.

"York gives me the same feeling," he said. "I appreciate his hospitality, no end. But there's some reason for it. Little things. Like giving a man pork when they know how any decent trapper would feel about pork-eaters."

"Maybe I made a mistake," she said. "Maybe I should have let Wachee kill you back there."

"I don't believe it was entirely due to feminine compassion that you didn't," he said.

Her breast lifted sharply beneath the canvas Mackinaw, and she stood that way a moment, biting her ripe underlip. She shook her head in a short angry gesture of restraint. Her voice was husky with the same restraint.

Then she said: "Perhaps you won't think this is due to feminine compassion, either. Maybe it isn't. Maybe I'd do the same thing for a dog. If I were you, I'd come in before night. Empty Pockets found those Cree shoe tracks down by the river this afternoon."

She whirled and moved back to the fort, the lilt to her walk turned to an angry swing. He watched her until she had disappeared into the fort. The same thing for a dog? He didn't quite understand. Had she meant it for a warning? Then her concern over Akomo was greater than she had shown. And this was to keep him from disappearing like the Indian. He had been about to boil his beer in the tank, but he turned to cover the barrel again, and then puttered about the still aimlessly for an hour or so until dusk began to fall.

With the light fading, he made his way down to the Missouri. There was something sinister about the constant undercurrent of cracking ice. He finally found sign. It was made by the same long-webbed racing shoe. It was hard to trail in the dark. He lost it several times. He kept listening for that owl hoot over the breaking ice on the river. Why should Benedict show like this? To contact him? The man must have some strong reason. Then, forcing his way through buckbrush on the trail, his eyes came to rest on the body, and he halted, the blood seeping from his face.

The *crackle* of bare bushes behind caused him to turn with a start, right hand lifting toward the Green River knife in his belt. Ione Napier stood there, staring past Shade to the decapitated body of Benedict in the snow. A sick expression twisted her mouth, but she continued to stare at the grisly sight.

"I told you he'd show up," she said. "Nothing but that *guayacán* of his could have done this."

"Akomo?" he said.

"Akomo."

VI

Two weeks had passed. Inside the fort Christian York was mincing again. His feet scraped the bare portions of the floor in a shuffle. He popped his lips out in that habitual pouting way, fingering them absently.

"The man in the Cree shoes," he frowned at the grizzly hide on the wall, "the man in the Cree shoes. What could that mean? Tell me what that could mean, Cameron?"

"Two weeks, and you're still worrying about it. How should I know what it meant?"

"Yes, how should you know? And Akomo. The woman said nobody could do a job like that but him, with that club of his. I'd believe her. I've seen him use it. But if he's alive, why doesn't he come in?" He postured back toward the desk. "That rumor of an American agent up here. But Cree shoes. That doesn't quite fit, does it? Following Wachee's party all the way north on Cree shoes. And why Fort Bliss? Why should he be watching us?" He turned toward Shade. "What do you think, Cameron?"

"I think you need a good pull on my sugar-top," said Shade, rising.

York brightened. "It's ready?"

"In them tarred barrels, and with a kick like a Hawkens rifle with a double load of Dupont powder. Delede helped me bring it in this morning." Shade had turned to open the door, and, as he swung back the portal, the undertone of sound burst on him in a hubbub. The outer room of the building was filled with buffalo-robed bodies and bronze heads with roached black hair. Half a dozen of the Indians were lined up in front of the counter with tin cups, and Delede was handling the bung starter on a barrel.

"Delede," called Shade, "I told you not to use that sugar-top for the trade whiskey . . . !"

Maybe it was the rusty barrel of a London fusil rifle, reminding him of the time he had seen one before. Or maybe it was the abrupt nod of a single eagle feather in another Indian's roach, as he turned his face, and the momentary glimpse of a hatchet profile that Shade had seen once and could never miss again. These were the Indians who had shot him up at Patchskin Buttes.

"Take it easy, Cameron," said York, from behind. "They're Hidatsa. They come in to trade once in a while and you don't dare offend them."

"I know they're Hidatsa," said Shade, watching the one with the face like a war hatchet start moving toward him, eyes narrowed, head thrust forward.

"*Canounye kicicupi,*" said the man abruptly, and Delede must have passed out several rounds, because his tone was thick, slurred.

"What's that?" said Shade.

"Something about war equipment."

York said: "Listen, Fox Dreamer. . . ."

"Fox Dreamer?" interrupted Shade.

The Indian spoke again, in a strange chanting way, turning his eyes toward the roof. "*To ke ya inapa nun we,*" he began, and the rest of it was lost in the growing welter of other voices as the other Hidatsa began to shift around behind the man.

"That's his war chant!" called York. "He's Fox Dreamer, Cameron, and that's his chant. Get back in here."

"Damn' right," answered Shade, because it was the same war chant he had heard back there at Patchskin Buttes when they had descended on him, and he saw other faces among these men that he had seen back there.

"*He walcan yan inapa nun we!*" shouted the Hidatsa, pointing his hand at Shade, and the rest of them began shouting and gesticulating.

"Can't you do something, Delede?" cried York.

"They're going to fight!" Delede shouted from somewhere. "I can't stop them, York. What have you done? They're going to fight."

"*Kola he ya ce e-e. . . .*"

"What have I done? What do you mean, what have I done? Get back in here, Cameron . . . !"

Fox Dreamer's rifle filled the room with its shocking detonation. But the Indians were notoriously poor shots, and the excitement and liquor didn't help any. Hot bark chipped off into Shade's face from where the ball struck undressed pine logs a foot beside him. Other rifles began to crash. They could have cut Shade and York to ribbons in that moment, but Fox Dreamer threw himself forward with his empty gun clubbed, followed by half a dozen of his fellows, and the others had to quit shooting for fear of hitting them.

York blocked Shade in the door, and the only thing the Kentuckian could do was throw himself forward. He ducked under Fox Dreamer's blow, and drove on in with an upward stroke of his Green River knife.

Fox Dreamer's fetid sweaty body was carried against Shade by its own impetus, held there a moment by the press of oncoming men behind, then allowed to slip down in an eddying shift of that press. The knife blade pulled free of flesh with a sucking sound, and blood dripped off its gutter onto Fox Dreamer's body, huddled at Cameron's feet.

Another body was thrust against Shade. He had the sense of leathery brown skin and teeth yellowed by tobacco and fanatical bloodshot eyes. He caught the flash of a knife blade and threw his free hand out to block the thrust. Then, with the Indian's wrist writhing in his left fist, he drove in once more with the knife.

"*H'gun!*" screamed the man.

A blow caught Shade behind the neck. Stunned, he released

the limp wrist and whirled, his knife held on a horizontal plane, edge out, belly high. Its wicked arc caught the man at Shade's flank. This one did not scream. He flopped backward with a sickly muted cry. Shade had the impression of spurting blood and crumpling legs.

The Kentuckian whirled back the other way with his knife in the same position. An Indian who had been charging in threw himself back from the flashing blade, face twisted, dropping his clubbed rifle. Shade found himself standing in a cleared circle, the body of Fox Dreamer and the second one at his feet. There was more gun clatter filling the big room. Other Hidatsas lay wounded or dying farther out. Past them, Shade caught sight of a grizzly pelt cap with its ear flaps turned up and a bulky red Mackinaw as Wachee, followed by Vide and some engagés, came in the front entrance, Hawkens rifle bellowing. The Hidatsa scattered to the four walls, dropping their weapons, shouting surrender. Wachee came on through, his rifle smoking in his hands.

"You all right, Christian?" he said hoarsely.

"Thanks to Shade, yes," said the fat man, standing in the doorway to the office. He fingered his fat lips, staring down at the dead Fox Dreamer. "But I wonder why they should have done this?" His eyes focused on Shade. "Eh, Cameron? I wonder why they should have done this?"

VII

Spring foliage had not yet come sufficiently to the trees. They still looked like skeletons to Shade whenever he looked at them. They still brought the thought to his mind of Akomo, stalking through them out there. The somber impassive face. The *guay-acán*. What did he want out there? Why didn't he come in and get it over with?

And there was the rest to oppress him. It was several weeks

after the fight with the Hidatsas. Shade was almost well, and still he had found nothing tangible to work on. He could get no information about Ojibway Fur's connection with the border trouble. It was like running his hands through smoke, seeking its source in vain. Wachee went out on trap lines twice. He did not bring anything back the first time, and the second time only enough to keep the half dozen *engagés* busy a couple of hours one morning, skinning and tanning. Whatever was going on, it wasn't trapping, but Shade couldn't find out what it was. He still made himself busy down by the still, but he couldn't keep his eyes out of those brooding trees.

Why don't you come in? It kept going through his head like that, along with the memory of Benedict's decapitated body. *Why don't you come in with that club of yours? I'm right here. Why sneak around out there and wait and wait and wait?*

And then one morning Wachee came down the slope from the walls of the fort. He stood a moment, staring at the still, scratching his dirty black beard.

"Really the little *bourgeois* now, ain'tcha?" he said. "Made liquor for the big *bourgeois* and saved his life and he just thinks you're the purtiest pelt in the bale." He shuffled a little closer, thrusting his head forward till his breath hit Shade's nostrils in a foul wave. "Well, I don't think you're so purty, Cameron. Just remember that. I still don't think you were poaching American Fur lines. Just remember that. I. . . ."

"Wachee, Wachee, that you?" The voice caused them both to turn. York was mincing down from the fort. "What are you doing down here?" said the factor. He didn't wait for an answer, turning to Shade. "We're off north, Cameron. I think you're well enough to join us, if you like. New preserves, and all that. About cleaned out of beaver down here. We need new trappers, if it suits your fancy."

The only duffel Shade had to pack was what few personal

articles had collected here. He put these in a possible sack and got Delede to issue him a couple of Hudson's Bay four-point blankets from company stock. In one of these blankets he cut a hole at the center, and slipped it over his head *poncho* style, pulling the four corners through his belt. Many an old whang hide preferred this type of garment to a coat, and with spring coming on it would suffice.

He felt no particular surprise when Ione joined the party gathering in the courtyard. She had her canvas Mackinaw on and a pair of black, river boots. Then the march started.

They moved north for several days on foot, always within hearing of that splitting, cracking ice on the Missouri. In a Mandan village they bartered brass kettles and lead shot for horses. Shade got a shaggy little piebald with a buffalo saddle. And always, each evening after the day's march, he would stare from the campfire into the skeletal shapes of the black timber surrounding the camp. The sense of the Tarahumare out there would come to him; he could feel him out there, waiting.

Shade did not know how many Sandy Creeks he had seen in his travels. This one was a tributary of the Missouri, turning directly north toward the Territories. It took them the better part of a day to reach its end. He knew they must be very near the border now. The country up here was bleak and desolate, even with coming spring. The timber of creek bottom petered out as soon as they left the end of Sandy. The horizon took on a barren aspect of rolling hills covered with short, greening buffalo grass. They reached a post at sundown, its walls of smoke-blackened pine logs rising abruptly from the desolate horizon. It did not look much like beaver country to Shade. Not enough woods.

The post had towers at each corner with slots in the walls, and a large cupola above the gate. They were hailed from here as they approached, and York went forward with Wachee to identify himself. Then the gate was swung open and the whole party entered.

Shade had seen some pretty motley crews in his travels, but this bunch made them all look like schoolboys on a Sunday picnic. It seemed as if every country had scraped the bottom of its barrel and dumped the scrapings down in this fort. They were a mixed lot. A weazened little man with a black patch over one eye had been playing a mandolin while half a dozen French *voyageurs* in white blanket coats and corduroys black with grease sang *"Le Chant du Voyage."* A dark, Gypsy-looking bunch with brass earrings and red bandannas around their hair, reminiscent of Portugee Houses down on the Powder River, stopped haggling over their game of monte for a moment. Shade had a quick impression of a man in striped British Navies with a slit ear, a tall attenuated Yankee in pale buckskins with a face as brown as the snuff he was taking, a trio of Mexicans in red *charro* pants over by the cooking pots.

"Christian York, by all the Cree gods in Athabaska!"

It rolled through the courtyard, drowning all the other noise. It came from the giant who had appeared on the porch of the main building. Sun and wind and weather had bleached streaks of pale gold through the red hair that fell in a shaggy mane almost to his shoulders, and the muscles lay in rolling slabs on his body, straining every stitch in his tattered elk-hide shirt.

"Tar Kelly," York told Shade. "Tar, I'd like you to meet Shade Cameron, a man of the versatile talents you would admire."

"A new recruit?" asked Tar.

"We'll see," said York, glancing slyly at Shade. "Let's go inside."

Wachee had already given his horse to an Indian and padded over to the card game, and Vide had joined his countrymen in singing. Shade accompanied York and Kelly into the main quarters. Tar pulled a jug off a shelf.

"None of that foul Indian grog," said York. "Cameron made us some real sauce." He fumbled in his duffel for the jug, looking up at Shade: "How do you like our little brigade, Shade?"

"They don't have many more trap scars than I do," said Shade.

A chuckle bubbled from York. "I guess they spend more time running American Fur men out of our preserves than they do trapping. What would you do, Cameron, if you were out on a line and found those renegades pulling up your traps and setting their own?"

Shade rubbed at his thigh. "I'd like to be there."

York's glance slid around to Tar, and he was still smiling. "I thought so. Cameron saved my life down at Fort Bliss, Tar. You should see him with a Green River knife."

"We can always use a good man with the traps," said Tar.

"Yes," said York with that secretive chuckle. "Let's drink to that, Shade. Then you can go out and get acquainted."

With the fumes of his corn liquor still burning his eyes, Shade left them. The hallway made a turn before reaching the front portion of the building. On one side of the main room was a long plank set on barrels, serving as the bar. Behind this were shelves of trade goods and whiskey; on the other side the stairway rose to a second story. Shade had to pass the foot of this to reach the front door. It was here he heard the voices from the landing above.

"Don't lie to me, Ione. You was going through them rooms. What are you hunting for?"

"Let me go, Wachee. I was hunting for my room."

"You knew where your room was all along. Not up here. What are you doing up here, Ione?"

"Are you going to let me go, Wachee? Do you want me to call York?"

"Go ahead. He'd like to see what I saw. Maybe I was wrong

suspicioning that Kentuckian. Maybe it was you I should have looked out for."

"Do you want me to call Shade?"

There was an empty silence. Shade heard Wachee draw in a heavy breath finally.

"That's different, isn't it?" Ione said.

There was another silence, then Wachee's voice, bursting out in husky vehemence: "No. Nothing's different. You tell me what you were doing up here or I'll. . . ."

"You'll what, Wachee?" asked Shade, having climbed enough stairs to see them beyond the turn in the landing.

The black-bearded man had forced her back against the wall. He turned his head without releasing her, his bulky red Mackinaw almost hiding the strained line of her body behind it. Then, slowly, his scarred hairy fingers opened around her wrist where he held it pinned above her head against the wall.

"Go back and tend to your own business, pork-eater," said Wachee.

Shade drew himself up a little. "Maybe it was you put that pork on my plate back at Bliss."

"Maybe it was," said Wachee.

"Maybe you better take it off again," said Shade.

"If you don't go back down those stairs and tend to your business," said Wachee, "I'm going to knock you down them and come down and break your neck at the bottom before you can get back on your feet."

"You still got a hold of her other hand," said Shade.

"Not now," said Wachee as he whirled, throwing himself bodily at Shade. The walls of the stairway were too close to permit dodging aside. Shade tried to duck in under. But Wachee's knee hit his chin, straightening him up, and then Wachee's whole body hurtled against him, knocking him backward. Shade went head over heels, shouting with pain as one arm twisted beneath him, unable to stop himself from flopping on down the steps. He glimpsed Wachee's body coming out of the dimness from above. The stairs rattled as the man came on down to catch Shade again before he stopped.

Shade twisted himself so that one shoulder went into the wall, stopping his body before the bottom step. Wachee tried to halt himself, thrown off by his miscalculation. But Shade twisted back up and lashed out with one hand. He caught Wachee's ankle and yanked. The man tripped and fell. Shade pulled Wachee on over his body. Wachee made an arc in the air above him, and then shook the building as he struck in the hall.

Shade got to his feet, grimacing with the pain of that twisted arm, staring down at Wachee. The black-bearded man lay on his back, breathing in a heavy stunned way. His eyes finally regained their focus, pinning on Shade. He rolled over, still looking at Shade, and got up on one elbow as if to rise. Shade leaned toward him, one hand slipping to his Green River.

"Yeah?" he said.

Wachee spat and got to his feet, swaying there. Then he turned and stumbled toward the doorway. Shade turned, rubbing his arm. Ione stood on the landing above. Her eyes were wide and dark. Shade and the girl stared at each other a moment.

"Well," he said finally, "did you find it?"

"What?" she said.

"What you were looking for."

"What was I looking for?" she asked him.

"Must have been something pretty important. Wachee was as excited as a country gal on 'tater day." He studied her face, trying to reconcile this new possibility with the utter lack of it in his former calculations. She had just been a woman before, a very beautiful woman with a deep bitterness toward Yankees and some obscure connection with York. But now. . . . "How many men do you think were in the courtyard?" Shade muttered, trying to remember what Benedict had said about British agents, their password. They add or subtract or something like that, knowing he was a fool to expect it, yet unable to restrain himself.

"About twenty-five," she said, and took one step toward him, a new intensity twisting her face. "And I've seen that many more inside the buildings."

"Making fifty," he muttered, and moved a step up toward her, a tingling sensation sweeping over him as he saw the possibility growing into a shocking fact. "And with me and Wachee and Vide and York. . . ."

He let it trail off, and her whisper took up the sentence, finishing it for him: "Would make fifty-four."

"How many do you suppose they'd leave at the fort when the brigade struck out for the trap lines?" he said hoarsely.

"Fifteen, maybe." Her voice was barely audible. She took another step down.

"I figure fourteen," he murmured.

"That would leave . . . forty . . . on the trap lines," she answered, her voice husky and strained.

"Fifty-Four Forty. . . ."

"Or Fight," she finished.

"You." It escaped him on a breath, and then he had taken that last step up to reach her, carrying her almost bodily back up the stairs and around the turn, holding her up against the wall.

"That's why those Hidatsas started the fight back at Bliss. They were the same ones who shot you up the first time."

He nodded, and her brows twisted in the effort to accept it all at once. "York thought American Fur men did it. That's one of the main reasons he accepted you," she said.

"Why do you think I let him believe it?" he said, his thin lips twisting in a humorless smile.

It struck him that he was holding her in the same position as Wachee had. Then something else struck him. It was the perfume of her hair, and then the soft feel of her body against him, and then his own desire for her, flooding up from months of lonely trails and womanless nights. His throat became tight, almost choking him. He moved back stiffly.

"That man in the Cree shoes was an agent, then?" she breathed almost fearfully.

"Benedict?" he said, and nodded. "The last of three agents the United States government sent up here last year. When he stopped sending in reports, they sent me out to find why. Benedict said the Crown had an agent out, too. He didn't know it was a woman."

"I'm not official," she said. "Dad was the one. He had been with Intelligence during the war. He'd been chief factor for Hudson's Bay Company at Bliss for seven years when this border trouble started. The Crown reinstated him and commissioned him to try and find out who was instigating all this. When he was killed, I took over."

"How about that Mexican Indian?"

She shook her head. "Akomo was with Dad. I told you that. He and I were the only ones left."

"What's he doing out there?" said Shade. "What's he waiting for?"

Again that shake of her head. "I don't know."

Shade's gaze sobered. "I guess you know how he feels about you."

Her eyes lifted, and she stared up at him, disbelief struggling with the dawning understanding in her face. "No, Shade. No. He was just Dad's man. Just faithful. They're like that, these ration Indians. . . ."

"You know Akomo is no ration Indian," said Shade. "And

you know how he feels about you. Is that why he didn't come in?"

"What do you mean?"

"He's a bigger threat out there than he'd be in here where we know what he's up to. Maybe he figures he can protect you better that way. I have the feeling of his eyes on me all the time. And that *guayacán*. Did he know what you were doing?"

"I don't think so," she said. "He never knew of Dad's commission."

"Just what were you doing?" he said, making a motion toward the opened door to their left with one hard hand. She grasped the hand, pulled him into the door. At first he thought they were bales of beaver pelts, piled against the wall. Then he saw a strip of red cloth pulled free of one, and the dim glitter of a brass button. He stepped over and tore at it. The bale came loose and a shako rolled out.

"British uniforms?"

"Enough to equip every man in this fort," she said. "And when they masquerade as soldiers and strike the next American post, the British army itself will be blamed."

His wheeling motion back toward her was deliberate, almost reluctant. "What post?"

"I've heard the name more than once this evening, among the men. Fort Renville. It's over by Devil's Lake. It's an old post. Settlers all around it. Women, Shade. Old people. Children. It will be the last straw. We'll have a war on our hands to make Eighteen Twelve look like a skirmish. . . ."

The words had spilled out faster and faster, her voice gaining intensity till it held a knife edge, shrill and biting. He realized she was up against him, clutching at his arms, hissing it into his face.

"You've got to get out and warn them, Shade. You're the only one. You ran the wood. If you ever ran before, you've got to now. They must be ready to move. That's why York came north. You convinced him you're the stripe to join him or he wouldn't have brought you."

"You'll come with me," he said. "We'll get a couple of those Mandan ponies. . . ."

"Don't be a fool," she lashed at him. "Think they'd let us just ride out the gates, the two of us, with not so much as a word? We wouldn't make it across the courtyard with those horses. You've got to go over the wall, Shade, you've got to do it all the way on foot."

"Let's go, then," he said.

"You!" she almost shouted. "I said you! I couldn't keep up a mile."

He stared at her, unbelieving. "You don't think I could leave you here," he muttered. "As soon as they find me gone, you'll be suspected. Wachee already has you in his black book."

"No, Shade, just because I'm a woman. . . ."

"Not just because you're a woman." He had her by the shoulders now. Perhaps it was the way he had said it, or what lay in his eyes. Her cheeks colored in a new understanding. His voice came out brittle, almost defiant. "Think I can't, if an Indian can? Think I can't, after being around you so many days, seeing you and hearing you?"

"Shade . . . ," she said, her lips twisting around the word in a strange, painful way. At last, she took a deep, shuddering breath, and then spoke in swift decision, as if forcing herself. "All right then. Even that way. You've still got to. What did Benedict die for? What did Dad die for? Just so a skinny corn-swilling Kentucky woods runner could have the whole thing in his hand and then throw it to the winds because he has spring fever over some girl?"

"No, Ione . . . no, not the way I feel. . . ."

"You've got to, Shade, you've got to. You're not a man, any

more. You haven't got any right to feel. You're only an agent. You've got the lives of thousands of people in your hand, and you're only an agent, and you've got to go."

"I can't, Ione," he groaned, "I can't."

VIII

A loafer wolf on some distant ridge filled the black night with his howling. A small breeze pushed its hesitant rattling way through greening willows.

Not a good friend, but a good agent, thought Shade, bursting through those willows, *not a good friend, but a good agent.* It kept going through his head, the way he had thought of Benedict when the man had left him to Akomo that time they had first met.

Shade figured he was about a mile south of the fort now. He had gone over the wall from the rear roof of a building. A sentry had spotted him running across barren ground and fired, without hitting Shade.

But that would start it. They would be coming out, British uniforms and all, knowing his significance now. There would be Ione, back there, and here he was, not a good friend, but a good agent, not a good lover, not even a man, just a machine, just a running machine to reach Renville ahead of them, back there, and the sick disgust filling him.

Are you smiling, Benedict? Shade ran down the icy shallows in an automatic effort to obliterate tracks. He could almost see the detached smile on the man's face. *Is this the way a good agent does it? Thousands of people, Benedict, I'm saving thousands of people. I'm preventing a whole war, Benedict. And they're killing her back there.*

He felt the tears running down his cheeks. He choked on a breath. That wouldn't do. He slowed down, struggling for more control. His lean legs were taut and knotty. He stretched out his pace. He was a youngster with Boone again, running the licks, coming through the Cumberland. He was in the tall birches of Kentucky, stretching out, with a four-foot squirrel rifle in one brown hand instead of nothing but a knife in his belt.

The sweat began to bathe him, loosening him more, oiling the stiff buckskins across the lithe movement of muscle. He was in the cactus of the Mexican Sierras, where he had first heard of the Tarahumares, and in the piñons about Santa Fé, and the pines of the Canadian Territories. He was in every stretch of timber he had ever run, running, running, running. And they had probably killed her back there.

Then, over that, or beneath it, or through it, came the dim awareness of something else. If he held his breath when he stopped, the pounding of blood in his ears would prevent his hearing. He allowed the breath to pass from him in a long, controlled sigh. At the very end of this expiration there was a moment when its sound ceased, and the beat of the blood in his ears stopped, and in this moment of silence he heard it.

No white man would make a sound, running, like that. It drew that terrible thin smile to Shade's lips, because he knew, now, what the Indian had been waiting for out here. He allowed his hand to brush the hilt of his Green River knife as he resumed his pace. *Where I come from, when two men race, they run till one of them drops dead and that is the way it would have to be with you and me, one way, or another.*

He got down into good timber by morning, big willows along the water, new green gleaming brightly in the first sun, taller pines blanketing a chain of rocky hills. Topping the first crest, he looked back. It took him a moment to discern the flitting motion through the foliage along the water of Sandy Creek below him. It was just a glimpse. But that an Indian would allow himself to be visible told Shade everything. It had settled down to the race, now, with no other considerations.

Shade struck the Missouri and followed its course southwest all afternoon. He was running heavily now. He still had control of his breath, and could see well enough, but the muscles in his legs were leaden, his feet grew heavier with each step. Renville was between the Missouri and Devil's Lake, and he veered away from the river with sunset.

With the disappearance of the sun, he was traveling through the night sounds again. The plaint of a wolf, the ominous *hoot* of a horned owl, the incessant swish of brush and grass with his passage through it. He stopped to wet his mouth, stifling the desire to drink. On upslopes he was slowed to a walk. On downslopes he was stumbling. He began to trip on things. Finally he went down. He knew an overpowering desire to remain there, sobbing with the painful heave of ribs. He forced himself up. Rising, he heard the farther *swish* of brush behind him. . . .

He could not see the morning when it first came. He was that blind. At last the light swam to him through his fuzzy vision. He was reduced to a stumbling walk now, spurting into a heavy dragging run only when that sound closed in on him from the rear, that inexorable Indian sound, that incessant, unvarying, deadly Indian sound that only an Indian could make in his run. Was the man inhuman? *Are you a machine? I'm done. I'm dead beat. Come on and get it over with. Come on in and get it over with. It's over. Can't you see it's over?*

But it wasn't over. He wasn't done. He kept stumbling on. Some dim spirit of Boone and the licks and the old shaggy Gap and all the other long Kentucky woodsmen behind him kept him going.

There had been other runs when he thought he was through. There had been that week on the trail with Ez. He tried to laugh with the memory of that, and couldn't get any sound past his dry, constricted throat. The trees spun around him. The tall spruce of the Territories. The blackjack along the Mississippi. The gnarled post oaks of a nameless land somewhere between the fifty-first parallel and the forty-ninth.

Noon sun blinded him with its brazen light. He slopped through sodden creek bottoms, falling on his face in the mud. He crossed high barren plains where a merciless afternoon wind cut at him like a Bowie knife.

Finally he stumbled blindly up a rocky slope through stunted oaks into slippery talus. He was almost to the peak when he heard the shale *crunch* behind him. He turned to see Akomo coming up through the surface rock in a dogged trot, pain turning his wooden face to a sickening putty color beneath the dark skin.

Shade turned, sinking to his knees in the grit, pulling out his knife. He kept his eyes glued to that advancing figure, trying to make it clear in his swimming vision. There was no strength left in Shade for subterfuge, and the utter doggedness of Akomo's stride made the Kentuckian think the Indian would have none left, either. Akomo came straight in, lifting that *guayacán* for the blow. Shade threw himself up off his knees straight toward the man, with the knife held at arm's length.

Suddenly he found himself past the man, knife going to the ground, arm crumpling up into his shoulder. That had been a feint on the Indian's part, and without striking down with his club he had side-stepped. Now he was back of Shade above his unprotected body. With an agonized gasp Shade jerked to one side. The obsidian on the club struck sparks as it hit the shale six inches to one side of Shade's head.

The Kentuckian caught the club as Akomo tried to pull it back. He gave a tremendous heave. The Indian would not release it. He was yanked down on Shade. The Kentuckian shoved his knife, point foremost, at the falling body. Akomo made a long sighing sound as the blade went in, and then his full weight fell on Shade.

IX

After a long time, Shade found strength to squirm out from beneath the body. The Indian lay, staring up at him, hands about the knife in his belly. It hurt Shade to draw in a breath for the word.

"Why?" he said on the exhalation.

"You were running to expose York," whispered Akomo, and little bubbles of blood danced on his lips. "I don't care what he was doing. I won't have her hurt."

Shade bent toward him, eyes wide, unwilling to accept the irony of it. Then he began to laugh—a thick, drunken, hopeless laugh. He saw the agonized question fill Akomo's eyes.

"You thought"—Shade choked on his laughter—"you thought she was with York? You were trying to stop me because you thought she was with York?"

"I knew someday you'd try to reach the Yankees with news of what York was doing," said Akomo, forcing it out in guttural pain. "I came to in that snowbank back on the Cannonball. At first, I thought of going on in and exposing you. But I had no proof, and York had always been jealous of me because of my position with Ione. I knew he would take your word over mine, if there was any doubt. I decided to remain outside and wait for you to make the break. Why do you laugh like that?"

"Because, you fool," panted Shade, "Ione is not with York. Her father was a British agent working to find out who had been causing this border trouble. She was doing the same thing."

The opacity left Akomo's eyes, and for that last moment a readable expression filled them. They shone in a final defeat. Then they closed.

Shade sank to a sitting position beside the dead man. He was stupid with exhaustion. The only thought that held any clarity was his knowledge that he had no will left to force himself farther. Akomo had won, after all. He stared dully about him without seeing anything. His gaze caught the lip of the crest. Then his eyes took focus. There was a plain beyond, covered with short, curling buffalo grass. And at the edge of timber on its other side stood the walls of a stockade, surrounded by squatting settlers' cabins. It was Renville.

The chief factor of the post that had once belonged to Astor's American Fur Company would not believe, at first, the story of the tattered incoherent Kentuckian who had crawled into the collection of houses on his hands and knees. He was a bluff, practical man, Captain Fenner, rubbing at a stubble of blond beard and studying Shade out of shrewd hazel eyes.

"You're crazy," he said. "Why should Christian York pull anything like that?"

Shade lay on a bench in the office of the fort, feebly trying to shove the company doctor away. "Ojibway Fur has been trying to get this section away from Hudson's Bay for years. Their first break was the Fort Bliss massacre that killed Napier and gave York the opening to take over there. There's rumor that Polk will settle for the forty-ninth parallel. If the border's drawn there, that will put most of the section York wants in the United States."

"We hope it does," said Fenner. "I've been working on the contract with Hudson's Bay down here. But most of my men are former American Fur men. They'd jump at the chance of getting a strictly Yankee charter."

"That's exactly what York figures," said Shade. "And where would that leave a Canadian company like Ojibway?"

"I know this is the richest fur section east of the Big Stonies," said Fenner. "But no man would risk starting a war just to get hold of it."

"You don't know Christian York," said Shade. "What he started in the Territories by merely pulling away from the Bay was practically a civil war. But maybe you do know Ione Napier."

"I knew her father, Paul."

"And her Tarahumare?"

"Akomo? I've seen him," said Fenner.

"Maybe you'd like to see him again," said Shade.

He could not walk. They had to carry him in a litter out to the rocky ridge. Fenner squatted down over the dead Indian with the Green River knife buried in his stomach.

"He followed me a long way," said Shade. "He wanted to stop me pretty bad. It wasn't just because he didn't like the shape of my nose."

Fenner looked at Shade. "He must have wanted you pretty bad, to follow you that far."

"How bad would you want me if you were set to start a war and knew the whole deal depended on me?" said Shade.

Fenner ran a broken thumbnail through beard stubble. "I've got twenty-four men."

"It'll be more than two to one," said Shade. "You'd better lay for him."

X

Most of Fenner's men had been with American Fur. There was a Yankee look to them, long and straight as a Hawkens barrel, brown as the ropes of shuck beans hung from a rafter in the Kentucky summer. They met Fenner's news without much talk, went for their rifles and shot, and came back ready.

Again Shade forced them to take him on a litter. They marched west, past the ridge where Akomo had died, into the timber beyond, and formed their ambush at the ford of a stream

Fenner called the Black Belt. Fenner put twelve of his men in the brush on one side of the ford, and a dozen strung out through the chokecherry thickets on the other.

They gave Shade a rifle and he crawled from his litter to sprawl beside Fenner. It was a new weapon, and Shade began rubbing dirt on the bright metalwork so it wouldn't flash in the sun and give away their position. The pain and exhaustion of his ordeal were stealing from him with the growing excitement.

"You promised now," he growled at Fenner. "The girl didn't have anything to do with it. Paul Napier was a British agent."

"If she's there, we won't shoot at her," said Fenner. "But I wouldn't set my hopes too high, Cameron. With all this lead flying, even if she is with them. . . ."

He let it trail off at the expression on Shade's face and turned to watch patterns of afternoon sunlight dapple the timber. It was almost dusk when one of the scouts came creeping back.

"Coming, sure enough," he said. "Every one in those red coats. Would have thought it a bunch of British infantry sure except for that tub of lard, York, riding a Mandan pony in front. Christian York and his whole outfit, Captain."

"The girl?" said Shade.

"Didn't see any women, Kentucky."

Shade's hand closed around the muddy barrel of his gun till his knuckles gleamed white through the taut brown skin. His whole body sank back against the ground, and he didn't look at either of the men. *Are you smiling, Benedict? Am I a good agent now?*

"Let the main body get out in that ford"—Fenner's gruff voice cut through Shade's thoughts—"even if a few skirmishers make it across before the big bunch, don't start shooting till we have the bulk of them in the middle out there."

The Yankee nodded and went away to pass on the captain's orders. Then it was the waiting again, with a night wind coming up as light faded. It was nearly dark when the first man appeared.

It was the ex-sailor. He was dressed in a red coat and shako now, but that slit ear was still visible. He moved in a tired jog that told how fast they had marched. His head moved neither to one side nor the other. He slopped into the ford, crossed it, disappeared into the timber on the other side.

In a few moments, the next scout appeared. One of the Portuguese, those rings gleaming dimly in his ears. After him, the sound of them came, the snort of a horse, the heavy tread of walking men.

They streamed into Shade's vision in a loose, undisciplined order. Christian York and Tar Kelly and a few others rode on a bunch of Mandan ponies in the lead. The rest of them were walking, looking uncomfortable in those red coats. Shade felt a tremor run through his body. One of the riders wore a red greatcoat with the sleeves dangling. It did not fit right, somehow. There was some kind of a bulge at the back. The figure was much smaller than the others. Or did it just look smaller, between Tar and York?

Shade felt Fenner's hand on his arm, and realized he was trembling. "Take it easy, Cameron, we've got them," said Fenner, and then that hand left Shade's arm and was raised, because the column was now filling the ford.

The shock of sound stiffened Shade. Watching that figure on the pony between York and Kelly, he had not been ready to fire with the others.

The whole column seemed to sway in and out, and then the muddy water was filled with red blood spreading in a thick tide from the red, crumpled figures.

"Load again," shouted Fenner over the last sporadic din of that first volley. "Load again, pick your man, get them while they're still in the water."

A good man with a Hawkens rifle could load five balls a minute, and the captain had hardly finished speaking before the firing began once again, more ragged now. Shade could see Tar Kelly above the general welter of disorganized men, wheeling his frenzied horse this way and that, trying to rally the men and drive them back through the fire toward the bank. Three of the Portuguese broke downstream. Two of them pitched onto their faces in the shallows of the ford. The water was up to the third's waist before he stiffened, head thrown back, mouth open, earrings glittering in the fading twilight, before he went under.

Shade held his fire, seeking Christian York in the mêlée. A Mandan pony went pounding past them through the timber, dragging a man in a white coat, his foot caught in the stirrup. It was Vide.

"Stay down!" bawled Fenner. "Stay down and give it to them! You'll lose the advantage if you don't keep it up now!"

But half a dozen of Fenner's men jumped to their feet, running on out with clubbed rifles.

Then Shade found York. The fat factor was on his feet in the reeling, swaying, screaming bunch of men out there. He had caught a figure by the shoulder and was driving it through the carnage toward a small point of black timber above the ford.

Fenner had planted three of his Yankees there, and Shade expected to see York caught in their fire. But they must have been among those who jumped out to engage in the hand-to-hand battles going on along the shore, for York met no fire. He kicked free of the bodies wallowing in the bloody water, spinning that figure on ahead of him. The greatcoat had come off now, and Shade could see what had made that bulge at the back of the small figure. Her hands had been lashed behind her. It was Ione, and her hands had been tied behind her.

"Cameron, stay down, you fool, you'll get killed out there!"

Captain Fenner's shout was lost beneath the animal sound

Shade made. His legs almost collapsed beneath him as he drove out of the foliage. He stumbled over a man all twisted up in a red greatcoat. He would never know how he managed to keep on his feet.

His whole body jerked and twitched with the force driving him. He felt none of the pain he should have. That awful lethargy of exhaustion was gone. His whole being was centered on those two figures almost at the timbered point.

He stumbled past three or four of Fenner's men tangled up with a bunch of Tar Kelly's men. He caught the flash of a clubbed rifle above his head, and threw up his own gun, dodging aside. There was the stunning *clang* of metal on metal. For a moment, he thought he had lost his grip on his Hawkens. Then he reeled on past, and the long gun was still in his hands.

At the edge of timber, York must have caught sight of Shade. He wheeled, a pistol rising in his hand. A figure got between Shade and York, a burly little bear of a man. Wachee's face, teeth bared savagely in his black beard, came into sight.

Shade had been saving that load for York, but he saw the rifle in Wachee's hands and could do nothing else. He had set the first trigger. The spring of the second was like velvet against his finger. The buck of the gun was like a kicking horse. Wachee's white snarl twisted. His eyes opened wide. The rifle twitched spasmodically at his waist, as if he were trying to drag it up anyway for a shot from the hip. Then he fell forward on his face.

York still had the pistol leveled on Shade. He must have been waiting for Wachee to get out of the way. Empty rifle in numb hands, Shade went on forward toward the man, staring, wide-eyed and helpless, down the black bore of that pistol. A sly smile fluttered York's swinish lips. Then the girl threw herself at the gun, her head knocking the barrel down as it went off.

The bullet slapped water at Shade's feet. He was that close.

He had run off ground into the shallows. York tried to wheel away toward the timber as he saw he had missed, but he tripped on the girl's body. Then Shade caught him from behind. All three of them went rolling into the muck.

York beat at Shade's face with the pistol butt. Shade reared up, jamming his rifle stock against the rolls of flesh in the factor's neck. York made a choked sound, grabbed at the rifle, twisted it from Shade's hand. Shade found himself rolled over beneath the oppressive weight of the man's body. He took in a breath, got water instead.

Choking, blinded, he groped for a hold, caught a finger in York's eye, rammed a knee at the man's crotch, fought in a terrible savage frustration to get from beneath the sprawled bulk. York's fist struck him fully in the face. The stunning pain left him powerless for a moment. He felt his hair grabbed, his head pushed under. The fear of drowning shocked him to life as more water choked him. He rolled over on his back, rearing up with York's hands still twisted painfully in his long hair. He could hear York's hoarse, winded breathing. He twisted around again, hair ripped out as he tore loose of York's grip.

Exhausted as he was, Shade's condition was still beginning to tell on the other man. York's breath bleated from his swelling throat like that of a grounded fish. His eyes bulged and a purple vein beat in his jowls. Shade got an elbow hooked around the man's neck, was surprised at the lack of resistance. He twisted one leg about York's knee. It carried the factor off balance.

Again they were in the water, Shade on top this time. Elbow still hooked about York's neck, he drove the man under. York shouted as the water closed over him, and it turned to a choked sputter. The great bulk twitched and jerked spasmodically beneath Shade. He sprawled his whole weight across the man's head, hooked elbow still holding York under. York made one last spasmodic effort to get out. In the desperation of knowing this was the final bit of force left in him, Shade hunched over that feebly bobbing head, forcing it farther under.

"Shade, Shade . . . !"

Shade's head raised, and he realized York was no longer struggling. Ione was crouched on her knees in the shallows, calling to the Kentuckian. He released York, crawled on his hands and knees to the girl. He got his arms around her, fumbling to untie the lashings, and she began to sob against his chest.

"They were going to kill me if you got through. Then they found Akomo's sign, following you, and York was sure he'd stop you. He said no one could outrun that Indian. It's been York all along, Shade. Even at Bliss. He wanted the post to work from down here. He didn't know Dad was an agent. He planted those dead American Fur men at the massacre to incense the British, the same way he planted that Hudson's Bay commission on the dead man at Fort Rice to fan the Yankees' anger."

"All right," mumbled Shade. He would have fallen if he didn't have her there to hold him up. "It's all right now."

He had the rawhide untied from her hands by the time Fenner came clopping over to them. The captain lifted York's head out of the water, dropped it back in.

"Dead fish," he said. "Some of them got away. Not enough to matter. I guess this thing is broken."

"I'm glad," said Shade, staring into Ione's eyes. "I want to stop being an agent. I want to start being a man."

Ione managed a faint smile. He had the idea she was staring at him so intently for the same reason he was staring at her, to lose, in her eyes, the sense of all that carnage about them.

"Fort Bliss would be a good place to start," she said.

"A man needs a woman," he said.

"I'll be there," she told him.

"I'll be there, too," he said.

★ ★ ★ ★ ★

WOLVES OF THE SUNDOWN TRAIL

★ ★ ★ ★ ★

From the beginning in his short fiction for magazines Les Savage, Jr. often preferred to set his stories in the period before the Civil War and avoid the 1880s. Even the early *Señorita* Scorpion stories avoid the 1880s by being set in the 1890s. His first published story, "Blood Star Over Santa Fé" in *Frontier Stories* (Summer, 43), is set in the period of the Mexican War, and his second, "Murder Stalks the Fur Trails" in *Dime Western* (8/43), has as its setting the period of the fur trade. "Wolves of the Sundown Trail," like his second published story, occurs during the time of the fur trade, but coming later in his career—it was first published in *Frontier Stories* (Spring, 49)—it has the added depth of character and historical background that had become hallmarks of his Western fiction.

I

Duncan Innes rose from the fire in a deliberate, unhurried way, picking up his Yerger rifle, and then he walked twenty feet into the trees. Here, in the black shadows outside the firelight, he dropped soundlessly into the screen of antelope brush and began loading his gun. He could not tell if he had actually heard a sound outside of the fire—after so many years in the wilderness, a man's sensitivities reached a more impalpable plane than that—he only knew that sense of a foreign presence had been brought to him.

His narrow, long face had the sharp, cutting thrust of a tomahawk, turning back and forth, first toward the Tetons, towering in bleak, lithic omniscience to the west of Jackson Hole, then in the direction of the Snake, where it flowed out of Jackson Lake. It had taken him two days to reach this camp from the place the mountain men knew as Colter's Hell, and some heretics insisted on calling Yellowstone. His elk hides were pliable with wear and grease and dirt against his long, loose-jointed body. He was perfectly relaxed, although alert, holding the latent force of a watching cat. Finally there was the rustle of brush under the purple foliage of alders across the open space.

"Trapper?" called someone from over there. It held the hoarse, grunting bestiality of a bear. "I come peaceful. You out there somewhere?"

If you come peaceful, thought Innes, *why are you hiding?* After another long pause, the man must have realized his obligation.

A shadow at first, a bulky, square-set shadow that moved like a bear, he shuffled forward on padded feet until light fell across his blackjack boots, his corduroy trousers, dark with grease, his coat made from the pelt of a cinnamon bear.

"Hell," he said, "you're as suspicious as a coyote. I'm John Ryker, and I come peaceful as a baby."

"Then tell your friends to show themselves," said Innes.

Ryker could not hide his mouth, parted in surprise. He clamped it shut, as if trying to mask the reaction. Then he chuckled throatily. "You got ears like some animal. Come on in, Wisapa."

The porcupine roach on the Indian's head and the black and white skunk fur, ornamenting his neck, marked him as a Dakota. A buffalo robe, worked with red and yellow quills, swirled around copper calves as he walked in and stood beside Ryker, leading a pair of saddle horses—one a buckskin, one a pinto—as well as a pack horse. His face was made up of bold, brutal planes, the flesh so swart it seemed almost Negroid. Innes waited another space, listening, sniffing, turning his narrow head from side to side. Finally he rose and moved into the clearing, keeping his Yerger on them.

"What's your business?" he said.

"No special business," said Ryker irritably. "Damn it, can't a man be sociable? I been up in the Wind River all winter without seeing a white man. I heard there was a Scotchman trapping down this way. I come fifty miles just to smoke a pipe. Mountain men are usually a wary lot, but I never seen one suspicious as you."

"Maybe you're the one who should be suspicious," said the trapper. "You're John Ryker? I'm Douglas Innes."

Ryker's heavy beard was almost as cinnamon as his bearskin coat, but it did not quite cover the subtle alteration about his mouth. "Oh." He emitted the word in attenuated understand-

136

ing. "Yes, I heard of you over in the Owl Creek. The original hard-luck kid. I even saw the body of your last partner. Something like that's supposed to happen to everybody connected with you. Is that the story? If lightning don't strike them, they get smothered in a snow slide." The hearty, throaty chuckle bubbled out of him again. "Well," he said patronizingly, "suppose I ain't superstitious?"

Innes shrugged. "Suit yourself. I've tried warning people all my life. I'm tired of it. I killed a buffalo yesterday. I've got some *doupille* left if you want some of that."

"That's better." Ryker grinned. "We'll supply the potables. Wisapa, get that Monongahela from our possibles."

The Indian fumbled through the Mexican *aparejos* they were using for pack saddles, bringing forth a couple of the flat, wooden kegs of whiskey the traders brought up from St. Louis every year.

Innes squatted down, beginning to spit the back fat. Shifting firelight seemed constantly to change the gaunt, dour planes of his face. His long, thin lips were clamped as tightly as a jump trap. Sandy hair fell to his shoulders, filled with dark streaks from wiping greasy fingers in it for years. Ryker threw aside his bearskin to hunker down by the fire, warming his belly. He wore a red, wool shirt underneath, and Innes caught the glint of firelight on the brass butt cap of an immense Ketland-McCormick, thrust nakedly through the man's belt. Something sly in the man's glittering, little eyes kept Innes taut, close to his rifle.

When Ryker passed the Monongahela, Innes meant only to wet his tongue with it. But the only liquor he'd had for years was the acrid Indian *tiswin,* and he could not help drawing deeply once he had the keg to his lips.

"There's supposed to be more than just that bad luck of yours," said Ryker. "A curse on your clan or something. I never did get the gist of it."

Innes found his painful reticence thawed by the fiery fumes of the Monongahela. "The Innes clan goes 'way back. I'm the namesake of Sir Duncan Innes, who fought beside The Bruce, back in Scotland. Alister Mor was one of those who opposed Bruce. In Twelve Eighty-Four, Bruce captured him and shut him up in Dundonald Castle on the Clyde. Sir Duncan Innes was put to guarding him. Alister pleaded with Sir Duncan to release him before he died of fever he'd contracted in the battle, but Duncan refused. On his deathbed, Alister pronounced a curse on Duncan, promising nothing but tragedy and death to any by the name of Innes, or any who should have association with them, until the clan Innes was exterminated. . . ."

He stopped, realizing the release he had allowed himself, and the firelight seemed to change his eyes from a deep-pooled blue to a sudden opacity that glittered like the reflection of sun on ice. Ryker grinned, handing him the whiskey again.

"Now, don't start getting touchy just because you've opened up to a stranger. A man needs to talk once in a while. That's probably your trouble. Surely there's no harm in telling someone his tales."

Innes shrugged, taking the keg. What was the difference? The man was right. He lifted the whiskey for a toast.

"Thumping luck and fat weans," he said, and choked on the burning liquid.

Ryker sent Wisapa an oblique glance. "So the curse came true?"

Innes nodded. "A bitter feud naturally arose between the Inneses and the MacAlisters," he explained. "Sir Duncan's son was killed on his wedding night by a group of MacAlisters. Sir Duncan's wife was carried off by a Viking sea raider. They both drowned in the North Sea. Sir Duncan's daughter had an idiot for her first baby. I could keep going on all night. Five hundred years of it, and not one Innes has escaped. After the Disarming Act in Scotland, a lot of Inneses and MacAlisters sailed to America, along with thousands of others. My grandfather settled in Virginia. A Tory named George MacAlister led a bunch of Hessians to my grandfather's plantation, and they burned it to the ground. Grandfather killed George with this very Yerger I'm carrying, and had to flee to Kentucky to escape his kinsmen. My father was born there and grew up to be a drunkard. He murdered my mother in a fit when I was sixteen. Grandfather killed him for it and in turn was hanged for murder."

"Lord," said Ryker huskily. "That's quite a story."

"You don't believe it?"

"I didn't say that." Ryker snorted. "Won't you let me express a little amazement? I've lived among the Indians too long to doubt anything like that. You'd be surprised at the crazy things I've seen. I'm as superstitious as they are, I guess."

"You speak awfully smooth for having been out here that long," said Innes, squinting at him suspiciously.

Ryker shrugged. "I come from college people. I'm not ashamed of my education. I even got Wisapa talking English as good as that of most white men on the frontier." He paused, studying Innes. "If that feud is still on, you'd better not go around Hoback Cañon. A man named Roderick MacAlister runs a trading post there."

"I heard of him," said Innes. "The son of George MacAlister was hunting my family in Kentucky. That's why I headed West after Grandpa was hanged. I can't see any sense in going on with this feud. I don't know whether Roderick MacAlister followed me or just drifted out this way. More than one of them did that. There's another MacAlister working for H.B.C. over on the Missouri."

"Suppose you found a man willing to be your partner, Innes?"

"He'd be a fool," said Innes. "If you saw the body of my last partner, it must have been in a tree. I left him with the Sho-shones, and that's the way they bury their own. His name was John Donn, and he was drowned in the spring breakup on the Wind. Another man threw in with me last summer, and the Crows got his scalp two weeks later. It happens to anybody con-nected with me."

"Knowing all that, suppose a man still wanted to throw in?" said Ryker. "Those Shoshones in the Wind River told me you'd been there, too, hunting for Lost River."

"Wasn't me," said Innes.

"Don't be like that," said Ryker. "They even told me that toast you made when you drank their *tiswin* . . . thumping luck and fat weans. A big Scotchman with a piece of parchment, hunting for Lost River."

"I told you it wasn't me," said Innes. "I haven't seen the Big Horns since 'Thirty-One."

Ryker leaned forward, his voice taking on a sarcastic tone. "Surely you've heard the Lost River story."

"Something about a Franciscan priest in the Seventeen Hundreds, wasn't it?" suggested Innes.

Ryker's voice thickened with that sarcasm. "Fray Escobar. Seventeen Fifty. He was an expert cartographer and kept an extensive journal on all his trips. These journals are preserved in documents of the Roman Catholic Church in Madrid and Mexico City. There's a legend that he got as far north as Colter's Hell, but historians don't hold with it, because there's no journals or maps to prove it. On all his travels, a Negro servant named Juanito accompanied him."

Innes could not help but glance at the dark Indian. The man nodded. His voice startled Innes, and the fluency of his English.

"Wisapa means Black Son in the language of the Dakotas. It is a story of my tribe that a white medicine man came into the Powder River country with a black servant many generations ago. When he left, an unmarried squaw had a child who was almost black. This child was my great grandfather."

Ryker pulled a small, leather-bound book from his coat, handing it to Innes. The paper was brittle, yellow parchment, with faded, partly obliterated writing in old Spanish upon it.

"Black blood wasn't the only thing Escobar and his servant left with the Dakotas," said Ryker. "He must have lost his journal there, too. It was one of Wisapa's fetishes, when I first met him, handed down through his family as good medicine. Turn to page fifty-three, about the tenth line, Río Perdido. It's under the date of March Tenth. Escobar says he's come upon the headwaters of a sizable river that was unknown even to the Indian guides, in a valley so close to being inaccessible that he stumbled into it by the merest chance. In one hour, sitting at breakfast, he counted ninety-eight *castores* . . . that's beaver, in Spanish . . . at a single pool alone."

Staring at the faded book, Innes could not deny the tug of excitement such a bizarre tale brought. "That's a dream. There aren't that many beavers left in all the mountains west of the Missouri. It's getting trapped out, Ryker, and you know it."

"But this river hasn't been found," said Ryker. "Trappers have been hunting it for years. With Wisapa's help, I've tried to find it. But the landmarks Escobar mentions aren't clear enough. The Indians had different names than he gave them, and a lot of them have probably changed since then anyway. Escobar drew maps for every other trip he made. He must have drawn one for this. Ninety-eight beaver in one hour at one spot, Innes. Think how that place must be crawling with plews. A man could get rich in one season."

"If you're still thinking of me," said Innes, "I told you I don't have any map."

Ryker's thick, hairy neck grew red, but he kept his voice low. "You'll never get it with that map alone, Innes. Together, we could find it."

"I told you. I don't have any map, damn it."

"Yes, you do. Give it to me."

Innes did not realize how much the whiskey had affected him until he tried to focus his eyes on what Ryker held in his hand. An iron pan resolved itself. A flat lock plate. A goose-necked hammer. A Ketland-McCormick.

"I tried to do it the friendly way, you'll have to admit that," said Ryker. He jerked the pistol. "Search him, Black Son."

The Indian threw off the robe, revealing the fancy buckskin covering his body, and rose softly to move toward Innes. Innes made a forward shift, as if to rise, but a wave of that pistol held him. Its threat was clearing his head some now. He could hear his own breathing. *Damn' fool, to trust anyone even a minute.* The Indian stooped to pull off his slipover elk-hide shirt. Innes reached up and grasped a wrist, lunging to one side with the grip. Innes heard the *click* of that goose-necked hammer, cocking under Ryker's thumb, but the shot would have hit Wisapa.

Innes tried to throw himself with the falling Indian, keeping the man between himself and Ryker, but Wisapa twisted in his plunge, and Ryker was leaping to his feet, reversing the pistol. Innes whirled toward him, trying to rise. Wisapa's hand hooked in his elbow, pulling him off balance. Ryker slugged with the clubbed gun.

It struck Innes in the face, and he fell backward with pain blotting out all perception. He felt the blow of the gun once more and knew he was lying on his back because there was pressure there. He heard Ryker snarl something, and felt hands pawing over his body. His moccasins were ripped off, his shirt, his pants.

"It's not on him," said Ryker. "Look in the pack saddle."

Stunned by the blows, Innes knew he could not hope to fight them. If they had gone this far for the thing, wouldn't they just as soon kill him? He had been a fool once tonight. No use laying himself open again by stupid heroics. Ryker had picked up his rifle in one hand and stuffed the pistol back in his belt. They were both going through his pack saddles now. Innes's feet were near enough to the fire. Summoning all his concentration in a supreme effort to overcome the daze of pain, he squirmed till his feet were right in the fire, and then swept them toward the horses. A shower of blazing sparks and *popping* sounds flew at the animals. They reared, screaming wildly. The Indian pinto charged right into the men bent over the pack saddles. Innes stumbled to his feet, plunging for the trees. He heard Ryker shout something from behind. He was in darkness when the shot came. The lead slug rattled through the purple flowers in the alders above his head.

He was dizzy and weak, and he reeled through chokeberry, ripping his bare legs, crashed into a cottonwood, gagged in the resinous scent of poplar. Somewhere ahead he could hear the rush of the river. He was going downslope. He could hear them behind, gaining on him. He fell in dark, loamy earth, rose to run again, swaying, stumbling, trying to shake the pain and giddiness from his head. There was a flash of white water in the darkness ahead. His feet sank in saffron sand. He knew he could not run much farther.

Spring floods were carrying all kinds of débris down the swollen river. Buckbrush floated past, soggy and matted. An uprooted aspen, still bearing clouds of yellow foliage, came into his vision. He waded out and caught at it.

Swirling water pulled him down. The sucking force of the tree caught his arms. He sank down into the sweet-smelling leaves, gasping painfully, and felt the tree gather speed. Deep water clutched at it, and for a moment he thought it would roll him off. But the foliage gave the trunk the stability of outriggers, and he was still solidly aboard as he passed out, that one last thought forming dimly in his mind, before all thought fled: *Thumping luck and fat weans, hell!*

II

The young woman had immense dark eyes, and the whitest skin Duncan Innes had ever seen. Her hair was blue-black as a Hawken barrel, caught up in laughing, tufted, wind-blown curls all over her head, making a wild, dancing frame for her strange, little, elfin face. Her mouth kept curling up at one corner in a smile, half compassionate, half mocking, as she bent over him. He tried to rise, but she pushed him back down.

"You'd better lie still for a while," she said. "I'm Nairn. My billie found you floating by our house on a tree yesterday afternoon. You're pretty sick."

"Your billie?" he muttered.

"My brother." She laughed. It was like tinkling glass. "Brahan."

"Nairn? Brahan?" Innes did not speak the names very loudly, because something was beginning to work in his consciousness, something dark with foreboding. He tried to find its logic. It was the Snake he had thrown himself into. Could he have been carried as far south as Hoback Cañon by that tree? Something inside him started crawling.

"I'm Brahan." A curly, black-haired, young giant beside Nairn smiled. "And this is Elgin, my older brother. And Roderick, my father."

"Roderick MacAlister?" asked Innes in a cold, dead voice.

Brahan's father must have been in his middle fifties. He was the biggest man in the room. Both Brahan and Elgin were over six feet, but Roderick topped them by the full length of his massive head. The deep, weathered lines of his open face were as stone-like, as uncompromising as the granite crags of the Tetons. His eyes were so blue they looked black, and he wore his mane of white hair down to his shoulders. His laughter at Innes's question shook the room.

"Aye, Lalland, how did ye ken a bouk like me was a Vic-Ian-Dhu?"

"You'll have to forgive Father." Nairn chuckled. "He's been here forty years, but he still talks like he came right out of Loch Shin. He called you a Lowlander, and he asked how a man like you knew he was . . . ?"

"I understood him," said Innes thinly. He was staring at the tartan Roderick wore, the hated colors of the MacAlisters. He could hear his grandfather cursing its red and green sett now; he could hear the Gaelic invective heaped upon its coat of arms by his father in a drunken rage.

"What's your name, trapper?" asked Elgin.

Innes got up before speaking, because he knew what would come when he told them, and something in his face kept Nairn from trying to push him back down. He saw that they were in a bunk room at the rear of a log building, its walls hung with the stuffed heads of bears, a huge moose thrusting its mossy antlers from the rear, the puncheon floor covered with bearskins and buffalo robes. He himself was draped in a red Hudson's Bay four point, warm and woolly against his bare hide. A silence had fallen in the room as they watched him. For a moment he thought of giving them a false name. The negation of that went through him so violently he shook his head with it. Despite the resignation the tragedies of his life had molded into him, some fierce pride of those ancient Celtic Highlanders still flamed within him.

"I'm Duncan Innes," he said.

There was a moment when all the sound in the world seemed to have stopped. Even his own breathing. He could see the diffused blood sweep into Roderick's face until the flesh looked crimson. A great pulse started a tom-tom beat across the man's temple. Innes grew taut, waiting for that roar of ancient Celtic rage to fill the room. It did not come. Roderick turned without a word and moved toward the door.

"Father," said Nairn. "Where are you going?"

"To git my claymore." Roderick could hardly force the words from his mouth. "An Innes should be killed with nothing else."

"No, Father . . . !" The young woman jumped after him, catching an arm. "You wouldn't . . . you can't . . . he's sick. Can't you see, a MacAlister would have more honor than that?"

"I have my honor." The shout was coming now, as deafening as the ice breaking up on Ben Nevis. "I won't allow an Innes in my house!"

"No, Father. . . ."

"Aye, aye!" bellowed the man, swinging her off his arm so that she fell against the wall. "I'm ard-righ here. I'm high chief. Do ye question my dictates?"

"Nairn's right, Dad!" called Brahan, going after him. "You can't do it to a sick man. Can't you forget this feud? We're in a new country now. We have no right to carry it on. This Innes never did us any harm."

"His grandfather killed my father in Virginia!" bellowed the man. "My own father died hunting them down! I'll do the same before I let one stinkin', crawlin' ferlie of them remain alive!"

He was in the other room now, the stamp of his feet shaking the floor, and Nairn and Brahan had followed him out. Innes could hear them pleading with the old man. He stood shakily, holding the blanket up about him, gripping the pine bunk post with the other hand, searching the room for some weapon. Elgin MacAlister stood near the rear wall, watching him closely.

He was a man about thirty, taller than Innes, with some of his father's massive size in his great neck, like a brazed tree trunk set on his shoulders, and the immense body structure of his thick-hewed wrists and great knobby hands. But the cease-

146

less animal movement of woods running or trapping seemed to have melted off all superfluous weight, until his frame bore the gaunt, drawn refinement of a timber wolf. His face, too, did not bear the full stamp of Roderick's stubborn, unbending integrity. It was narrower through the jaw and brow, something almost sardonic in the tilt of his black brows.

"Never mind looking for a weapon," he said. "Nairn will argue him out of it. She's the only one who can handle Dad. It's unfortunate, in a way. I think you should be killed."

Innes looked sharply at him. "Isn't that unreasonable? Just because I'm an Innes? I never saw you before. I never did you any personal harm, and you never did me any, and, if we met under other circumstances, there would be no cause for a quarrel."

"But these aren't other circumstances," said Elgin. "To a true Scot, the honor of his clan is as precious to him as his own name. It doesn't matter that Sir Duncan Innes killed Alister Mor over five hundred years ago. I could feel no more cause for vengeance if it had been you killing my brother yesterday. If you don't see it that way, you aren't worthy of being called a Scotsman."

"Oh, now, Elgin," pouted Nairn, coming into the room with a tray of food. "Here we've just got Father quieted and you start. Can't we have peace? I've brought Innes some food. Let's toast to a new day in the history of our clans, a day of friendship and good will. Here's health to the sick, stilts to the lame, claise to the back, and brose to the wame."

The brose was potage made by pouring boiling water over oatmeal that was stirred while the water was poured, and the wame was the belly that Innes soon filled. With the oatmeal were square cakes Innes had heard his grandfather call bannocks, and a broth Nairn said was broo. Brahan came into the room while Innes was eating. He bore the candid, open honesty of his father in his red-cheeked face with none of the older man's stubbornness. Like a big, clumsy puppy in his movements, he seated himself casually on the floor beside the bunk.

"Father's cooled off now, I guess," he said. "Tell us how you happened to be floating down the Snake in such a naked state with big weals on the back of your head, Innes. Did somebody rob you?"

"Just as well," said Innes somberly. "A man named Ryker was trying to get a map from me that I never had. He said a Scotsman had been up in the Big Horns with an old Spanish map, hunting for Lost River."

Brahan looked in a surprised way at his sister. Then he reached inside his red wool shirt to pull forth a roll of buckskin. When he had opened it, there was a dirty, faded piece of parchment.

"That was me, last spring," he said. "I saved the life of a Franciscan father down near Santa Fé two years ago. He gave me this. I told him I didn't want pay for such an act, but he forced it on me. Said it had been in the possession of the chapel at Chimayo for a hundred years. It would do a fur man more good than a priest. Dad didn't take any stock in it. But I was trapping north last spring, and I turned aside for a couple of months."

"Did you find Lost River?" asked Innes.

"No." Brahan frowned. "But I found plenty of evidence and stories among the Indians up there to prove this isn't too far off the track."

"And you're a damned fool for showing anything like that to an Innes," said Elgin. They all turned to him, and an empty, uncomfortable silence filled the room. "What's the matter," he asked mockingly. "Am I not even welcome among my own kin? Time was when an Innes would never have crossed our threshold. Now, one comes in and takes my place!"

"Oh, don't be bleth'rin' like that, Elgin." Nairn sighed. "Can't we treat him like a human being? Can't you forget all that?"

"No," said Elgin, looking at Innes. "Never."

III

The days passed too swiftly for Innes after that. Because of Nairn. She brought him all his meals and sat often late into the evening, talking with him, sometimes in the buckskin skirt of the trading post, sometimes dressing up for him in the plaid and arisard of her clan. She took up one of Brahan's shirts for him, and found a pair of elk-hide leggings with all the fringe cut off by some trapper for whangs. She talked brightly the first day or two, keeping him amused with her news of the early spring rendezvous on the Green that Brahan and Elgin had attended, with light chatter about her own history, her childhood, her trip West with her father, the founding of the Hoback Post.

But he sensed a definite attempt to keep it impersonal, a maternal desire, perhaps, to shield him from anything somber or depressing during his convalescence. It was ironic, in a way, for that would indicate that she felt any discussion of his own past could be nothing but somber. Finally, however, on the third evening, she could not control her natural curiosity. She sat beside his bunk in the silence that had fallen, and he could feel her eyes on him. He lay on top of the blankets, arms behind his head, listening idly to the sounds Roderick made in the front room.

"You're a strange, morose sort of man," she observed then. "More like the old Highlanders than most third-generation Scots. Yet you don't even speak like a Scotsman. What makes you this way?"

"Maybe I'm naturally so," he murmured.

"I can't believe it," she said. "Not to such a degree. Only an animal that has been hunted and hounded and cheated and hurt all its life is suspicious and secretive. You remind me of that, a lot. Is it the curse? Has it followed you that closely?"

He looked darkly at her. "Most men would ridicule it."

"I'm a Scot, Innes," she said. "And a MacAlister. I've heard it all my life. I've seen it work. My father showed me the ruins of your grandfather's plantation when we were passing through Virginia. I was ten when we heard a man named Innes had murdered his wife in a drunken rage in Kentucky. I was with Father when he traveled there, seeking your people out of vengeance for George MacAlister." She caught at his arm, bending toward him. "It can't go on like that forever, Innes. It's got to stop somewhere. Maybe this is the place. The first time an Innes has been in the house of a MacAlister for over five hundred years. You don't know how hard it was to win Father over. I didn't realize I had that much influence on him. But it's happening, Innes. Let me help you."

He turned part way on his side to find that she had bent toward him so closely that his own movement brought their faces to within an inch of each other. The smell of her was too much like heather, the look of her too beautiful. He realized how long it was since he had been this close to a woman. A man got lonely, and the craving took on an intensity that was painful sometimes. A tremor ran through his body, and he found it hard to get the word out.

"Why . . . Nairn?"

"Why?" She shook her head from side to side, lips parted with the word, as if trying to find the answer herself. Her breath warmed his face, full of a faint, seductive scent. Almost as if it were not his own volition, his arm went about her, and he rolled over until the upper part of his body was against her, his legs slipping off on the floor to give him leverage, bending her backward in a kiss. She took it with no resistance, a growing eagerness in the way her lips ripened against his. When he finally took his mouth away, they were both breathing heavily. She stared up into his eyes for a long time, without speaking. Finally it came in a husky murmur.

"Now, do you have to have a reason why I should want to help you, Innes?"

He turned violently toward the wall. "Go away, Nairn. Before it's too late. Nobody's ever been associated with me who didn't suffer for it. I couldn't do that to you."

"Maybe it's already too late, Innes."

"It can't be," he said viciously. "Forget what happened. It could happen to any man and woman. Just a kiss."

"It's more than that to me, Innes. The kiss is just a proof of it."

"No," he said in a tortured, almost incoherent way. "Not with me. I've kissed a lot of women. Never meant anything." He turned his head away.

"Then why does it bother you so?" she said.

"It doesn't," he said. He wouldn't face her. "Go away, will you, Nairn? Leave me alone. Please."

She left him, then, there in the darkened room, and it was the first time he had ever wanted to cry since he was a child. He had never craved anything so badly—and had never seen so little hope of attaining it.

He tried to avoid her next morning by getting outside. But she found him down by the creek. The wide, frank depth of her eyes on him was a challenge. He tried to avoid it, skipping rocks, hunting for beaver sign, pointing out the tracks of a pronghorn to her. But all the time, her eyes were on him, and he could read the feeling in her easily enough, because the same thing was in him. The men felt it that night at supper, and it was a strained half hour, with Roderick leaving the table in a surly mood. Innes retired early to escape her, but could not sleep. The next morning he told her he had to leave.

"Why?" she said in a small, hollow voice.

"If I stay much longer, I won't be able to leave. I couldn't do that to you."

"You're talking about your feelings for me now."

Her voice was stronger.

"No. . . ."

"Yes. Why don't you say it out loud, then, instead of beating around the bush? I'll say it, if you won't, Innes. I love you."

The shock of it stopped him for a moment, and then his voice left him in a guttural, strangled sob. "No, Nairn, you can't let yourself. . . ."

"I can't help myself."

"It's just being around so close to me. A stranger. Something new. You don't get many men here. Just your brothers. When I'm gone, you'll see."

"I should be insulted," she said. "You don't know how many men have courted me, Innes. One came three hundred miles. I've known enough men. I never felt anything for the others. I do love you. I told you. Do you love me?"

The quiet, candid depth of her gaze went clear down to the bottom of him, and he thrust his head from side to side in a tortured way. "No, Nairn, I can't let myself. . . ."

"It's time you stopped running from that curse," she said. "You've been running from it all your life. You ran from Kentucky when your mother was killed. You haven't stopped anywhere along the way to fight it."

"But I have. I have, you don't know how many times. . . ."

"Then stop again. We're already fighting it, Innes. You're living in the house of a MacAlister."

"With Elgin waiting to kill me and your father hoping for one false move?" he said bitterly.

"Are you afraid of them?"

"No," he muttered.

"Are you afraid of me?"

"No."

"Do you love me?"

He stared at her, the contortion of his face twisting all its flat, hard planes out of shape. He couldn't tell her. He couldn't suck her in like that, draw her down, lay her open to what so many others had suffered. The conditioning of a lifetime blocked him off from it. He drew in a warped, rended breath. Then, slowly, he forced a grin onto his face, emitted a harsh, cynical chuckle.

"Don't be a *fule*, kid," he said, mocking her with the Scottish word. "Sure I'm thinking of the curse. I'm trouble, and you can't get out of it. But not because I love you. I'm fond of you. I'm grateful to you for what you've done. And for that very reason I'm leaving. I'd do the same for a dog. I'd kick him away from my campfire for fear a bolt of lightning would strike him there or a MacAlister would shoot him for being with me." He saw the stricken look fill her eyes and squint them, as if with the shock of pain. He turned swiftly away, unable to bear it, and walked swiftly to the door. The front chamber comprised the store of the trading post, with a long plank set on barrels sufficing for the counter. It was filled with scents of acrid, black powder and sour leather and stored pelt. Roderick was standing behind this plank, and he must have heard them, for he put his two massive hands on the board, and it groaned as he leaned his weight forward onto them.

"So you're leaving," he said. "Good riddance to the devil, I say. You're going that way, with not another thing from me."

"Dad," said Brahan from the doorway, "at least give him a coat and some food."

"Shut your trap, you crawlin' ferlie!" shouted Roderick. He beat one hand on the plank, causing it to clap sharply against the barrels at either end. "I'd rather he left feet first, but I gi'e me word to Nairn. Just remember that, ye ree, chuffle-mouthed brak of an Innes. Gin ye leave that door, the promise is over. Gin ye ever show up again, I'll take me claymore to ye!"

"Guid swats," murmured Elgin. He sat in a dark corner, peeling an apple, and Innes had the feel of the man's sardonic eyes on him all the way out. Brahan followed, slipping out of his heavy coat of Scottish plaid.

"Here. It's spring, but you'll need it. I've got a rifle and some shot if you'll wait a minute."

Innes started to protest, but the young man was already in his clumsy, puppyish run toward an outbuilding where he slept, returning with an old Jake Hawken and a shot pouch and buffalo horn.

"I'll pay you back somehow," Innes told him gratefully.

"Don't insult me," said Brahan, laughing, clapping him on the back. "We're brother Scots, aren't we?"

That warmed Innes unaccountably, and he felt himself turn his face away in a paradoxical, typically masculine gesture of embarrassment in the face of sentiment. *How strange a man got when he stayed away from his fellows,* thought Innes. Here, the most he wanted to do was thank Brahan, and yet he could find no words to do it with; he could only find an embarrassment so deep it blocked up his throat. Brahan put a hand on his shoulder and told Innes he would accompany him to the mouth of the cañon.

They set out toward the trail along the river bottom. Before plunging into the thick willows, Innes glanced back once. Nairn stood in the doorway. Her face looked small at this distance, doll-like, a cameo of lost, hopeless pain that twisted his insides till he thought it was a cramp.

Spring was ripe in the land now. Scarlet cones covered the upper tips of the spruce, and they stood like flaming pyres against the darker green of pine and fir. The aspen crowded the sandy banks of the Hoback River with fluttering jade, and the red-blossomed balsam poplar filled the air with its honeyed scent. The rusty coat and double-prong antlers of a mule deer flashed through the willows, and great, soft eyes peered at the two men for a moment. Finally they reached the columnar ochre cliffs forming the cañon mouth.

"You want to keep an eye out for Ryker," Brahan told Innes. "I was down to Bridger's Fort while you were sick. He was there with that Dakota of his. I even had a few words with him."

"You didn't have a fight?"

"No," said Brahan. "But I told him he picked the wrong Scotsman when he thought you had the map. The next time he wants a look at it, he'd better hunt up the MacAlisters."

"You fool!" said Innes. Then he quieted, staring, narrow-eyed, at the man. Finally he brought himself to speak. "You did that . . . for me?"

Innes saw the same embarrassment in the young man he had felt earlier. Brahan shrugged, grinning self-consciously. "You won't be bothered any more."

"But you . . . ," said Innes, "you've laid yourself wide open. He might try it again."

"We have a saying in our house," Brahan told him. "It's ill getting the breeks of a Highland man. In this case, Ryker will have to get the britches off three Highland men. Dad and Elgin and I may have differed over what to do with you, but when it comes to a fight, we stand as true as a Lock Liel oak."

Innes started to say something, broke off. Brahan must have sensed his inhibition. The youth thrust out a hand, and Innes took it gratefully, feeling in the firm, strong grip all he could not express vocally, knowing Brahan understood now.

Without speaking again, he turned and made his way over the pale buffalo grass to the sparkling confluence of the Hoback and the Snake. He ducked into timber, hunting a ford, and was deep down an avenue of spruce when he heard the sharp report. He halted, thinking it might have been ice breaking up on the heights. But that did not suffice, somehow. In a dark, Celtic premonition, he turned back. He was running when he reached the edge of timber, turning up a slope that brought him out on a bluff above the spot where he and Brahan had halted.

The men must have been a quarter mile up the cañon. Two of them were dragging Brahan's body from an open glade into timber. A cinnamon bearskin caught the sunlight in ruddy tints. There was no thought in Innes's mind at that moment. He was flooded with a terrible, blinding anger that clogged up his throat with hot blood and started the pulses across his temples to pounding like drums. He threw himself down the bluff, sliding through shale and chocolate earth, landing heavily on the slope below. Then he began to run, loading his rifle as he went, in a thoughtless, mechanical way. He was sucking in great, painful breaths from the long, punishing, uphill sprint when Ryker's head turned. They had dragged Brahan within a few feet of the willows. Ryker dropped the slack body and wheeled. Apparently he had not stopped to reload after shooting Brahan, for he plunged into the trees without trying to fire.

Innes took a snap shot at the disappearing bearskin coat. Wisapa followed Ryker, and the two of them were gone. No woodsman in his right sense would have run after them, crashing through the underbrush, but the rage was still so roaring in Innes that he had no caution. He ran for 100 yards without even trying to cut sign and found himself at the river. Then, gasping painfully for air, vision swimming with exhaustion, he realized he had about played out his string.

They were nowhere in sight. He backtracked, trying to pick up their sign, but his own passage had obliterated whatever tracks they had left. It would have taken him an hour to unravel their sign from his for any distance. He finally went back to

Brahan, sobbing with the terrible frustration of his defeat, hands working on the rifle with an awesome rage filling him.

The youth had been shot through the back, and was dead. His shirt and pants had been searched, and Innes knew why. A few feet into the open, he saw the large sheet of tanned buckskin Brahan had wrapped the map in. Then the steady plod of running feet entered his consciousness, driving him upright. Elgin and Roderick appeared on the river trail, coming at a steady dog-trot that any woodsman worthy of the name could keep at for hours. Innes's figure, rising up beyond the band of willows, must have caught Elgin's eye, for he turned, and then plunged toward Innes. He halted when he was near enough to see Brahan on the ground. Roderick came up, staring at his son.

Then, in ominous silence, the two men began moving forward again. The red fireweed *swished* at Elgin's buckskin leggings. The blue asters whispered around Roderick's laced boots. The river made little chuckling murmurs in the distance. Innes watched them in a strange, petrified tension, unwilling to think, a horror growing in his eyes as he saw what lay in Roderick's face. Elgin knelt beside Brahan, feeling for his heart through the bloody shirt.

"Dead," said Elgin in an empty tone. He turned to look up at Innes, a curious lack of emotion in his voice. "We heard the shot from the post. I told him he was a fool to show you that map."

Roderick made a small, animal sound in his throat, and started walking toward Innes. "My son," he said. "Ye killed my son, Innes. I might hae kenned it. An Innes. And I took ye in, Innes."

He kept saying the name over and over again, as if it were a curse, something blasphemous. His great, knobby hands lifted in front of him. Innes stepped back, raising the gun with an instinctive, defensive gesture.

"No, MacAlister," he said. "No. It was Ryker."

"Who's Ryker?" said Elgin, rising from the body.

"Stop, MacAlister!" shouted Innes. "Let me explain!"

"Ye'll do yure explainin' to the de'il!" roared Roderick, and jumped at him.

In that last instant, Innes realized he had been too deeply in his anger even to reload the gun after that first shot. He did not think he could have fired anyway. One of Roderick's fists knotted up and lifted for a blow. Stumbling backward, Innes brought the Jake Hawken across in front of him to block it. The man's fist hit the rifle where the iron barrel joined the stock. There was the sharp splinter of wood, and the gun broke into two pieces, and that fist came right on through to smash into Innes's chest.

Innes heard the hoarse, agonized exhalation he emitted. The pain seemed to fill his whole being in that instant. He had a sense of his whole body crumpling up. But instinct was still jolting him, and with the conditioning of countless other battles like this he rolled his body to one side and hit, going over and over on the ground, away from Roderick.

He had a dim vision of Elgin, stooping to grasp the barrel half of the rifle and lunging after him with the deadly iron pipe raised as a club.

Coughing in a deep, sick way from the pain of that blow in the chest, Innes made a feeble attempt at rising to his knees. Roderick was coming at him again, and would reach him before Elgin. With that flashing glimpse of their two faces, Innes got an instantaneous impression of the crazed, insane light filling Roderick's eyes, and the cold, calculating lack of emotion in Elgin's.

Then he had twisted around, not yet fully risen, to dodge Roderick's next blow and lunge in under it against the man's legs. The length of his torso thrown against the man's knees upset Roderick, and he fell across Innes. As the giant Highlander went down, one of his great, clawing hands caught Innes's arm, pulling Innes back down off his knees onto the ground.

With both of them wallowing across the buffalo grass, Innes saw Elgin leaping around to put himself in position for a blow. In a terrible, feeble desperation, Innes caught at Roderick's arm, hooking in under the elbow and pulling the man's great body across him. Roderick came willingly, clawing for a grip with his free hand, gasping Gaelic curses. Elgin could not abort his blow soon enough, and the length of the barrel struck Roderick across the thick muscles of his upper back. His sick grunt of agony beat hot and fetid breath across Innes's face. His massive body sagged heavily against Innes.

Innes caught the rifle barrel before Elgin could lift it again. Elgin tried to pull it free, and Innes used the opposing force of that to pull himself from beneath Roderick's great, stunned body. Roderick pawed feebly at him. Innes kicked the man's hand free. He felt the rifle barrel slipping out of his hands, with Elgin's savage jerk, and let go completely.

Taken off guard, Elgin stumbled backward, trying to regain his balance. Innes threw himself at the man, butting him in the stomach. Elgin gasped and went down. Innes went with him, straddling him, beating at that dark, sardonic, mocking face with all the strength left in him.

He heard Roderick's groaning behind him, and knew he was trying to rise. Then he heard Nairn's voice from the river, and turned to see her stumbling up the trail. She must have been left behind, unable to keep up with her father and brother in that dogged run, for she was gasping, her face flushed with the terrible exertion, her arisard torn by brambles, her black hair wild about her face from the wind. She caught at the low branch of an alder and took in the scene with one swift, understanding glance.

"He killed Brahan," groaned Roderick, now on his hands and

knees, shaking his head like a great, dazed bear. His shirt was bloody across the back where that blow had caught him. "He killed my son."

"No, Father," said Nairn desperately. "He couldn't have. He wouldn't do that."

When Innes got up off of Elgin, the man rolled over, pawing at his face and moaning softly, trying in a weak, half-hearted way to rise. Roderick saw Innes get up and started coming to his feet.

"Don't, MacAlister!" Innes cried at him. "I don't want to fight you like this. Damn you. I didn't kill Brahan. I don't want to fight you. There's no reason for it. Don't, please . . . !"

With a small, despairing sound, Nairn threw herself in front of her father. He tried to swing her out of the way, but she caught at his torso, winding her legs into his. Still dazed by that blow, he tripped again and went down on her. Innes heard her cry of pain as his weight pinned her to the ground, but before he could reach them, Nairn had squirmed from beneath Roderick, throwing herself across him to hold him down.

"Leave, now," she sobbed at Innes, her face flooded with tears of utter desperation. "Please go. You'll have to kill him to stop him, and, if you don't do that, he'll kill you. Oh, please, Innes, get out, go away, while you've got the chance."

Innes stared for that last minute at the pitiful, sobbing figure sprawled over the gigantic Scotsman. A terrible despair shook his whole frame. He heard the sibilant brush of Elgin getting to his feet behind him and knew that he did not have the strength left to face them both again. The sound he made as he turned away to plunge into the timber was hardly human.

It seemed as if he had been the repository for all the tragedy and death his clan had known for the past 500 years, and it had lurked somewhere down in the dark depths of his unconscious, waiting for the culmination of this moment, to sweep up and inundate him with the terrible, devastating, final defeat of his inheritance.

IV

The summer sun made a brilliant glitter on the ice fields of the Wind River. The trunks of aspens traced their delicate silver columns against the dense green of pine on the slopes. Goldenrod looked like patches of yellow sunlight against the curing buffalo grass filling a glade. There was a furtive, darting movement amid the spruce at the edge of this meadow.

It was a man, crouching in the yarrow, plucking at wild strawberries in swift desperation. There was not much humanity left to him. All the marks of the wild, hunted animal stamped him. He had no shirt, and his scarred, gaunt torso was burned the color of mountain mahogany by the sun. His feverish, sunken eyes were never still in his narrow skull, shifting back and forth like the dance of light on water. His mouth was hidden in the matted, sandy beard obliterating the long, bitter line of his jaw. He had been wild and shy enough originally. Now, few would have recognized him as the Duncan Innes of four months ago.

There was a *snap* of underbrush from across the glade, and Innes leaped back into the brush, crushing the berries in his hand till the juice ran red as blood from between his fingers. Deep in the thicket, still running, he turned to look over his shoulder. A brown bear had ambled into the glade, rooting for wild onions. Innes halted himself with great effort, making an angry, snarling sound, and dropped on his hunkers to stuff the crushed mass of strawberries ravenously into his mouth.

The juice dripped into his beard and ran heedlessly onto his chest. The hair on the top of his head was almost white from the sun, and almost black on the sides and back from using it to wipe his hands whenever he ate. He added to that now with a swipe of wet fingers across it.

He caressed the bare blade in his belt for a moment, considering the possibilities of getting the bear with that. It had been two weeks now since he'd had meat. The last had been a rabbit, caught in a deadfall after days of patient trailing and waiting. He shook his head finally, realizing how foolhardy it would be with only a knife. There wasn't even a hilt on it. He had found it in a rotting trapper's cabin over in the Shoshones. How long ago had that been?

He looked over the glaciers above and behind him. There were no known trails over the Wind River. He had followed a game trace made by mountain sheep, and had gotten through by chance. He shivered with the memory of the freezing night, clambering over ice fields, almost falling into a crevice so deep he had not been able to see the bottom. There were many lucid moments like this, when his mind would work with some logic. But there were other periods he could not remember at all, when he must have run like some animal, aimlessly, thoughtlessly, sleeping when he felt the need, eating when he could find food. Brahan still came to his mind, occasionally, and he felt a resurgence of that terrible defeat. Mostly, though, it was an apathy. He felt no desire for anything beyond the fundamental necessities.

When his shirt had fallen apart, he had not cared about mending it, or getting hide for another. He found within him a growing aversion to human beings, almost a fear. He had assiduously avoided a party of trappers sighted two weeks before. And beneath it all, haunting him, driving him, harrying him till he could never stop moving, like an animal running from the hounds, was the knowledge that he was being followed. He knew Scotsmen, and he knew Roderick. The man would not let the death of his son go unavenged. The man was on Innes's back trail somewhere, stubbornly, ungivingly, patiently sifting out his sign and plodding along after him, inexorable as the curse itself.

Innes rose and started downslope once more. In his mind was a vague idea of reaching the valley before nightfall. It would be somewhat warmer, farther from the ice that never melted up there in the glaciers. Beyond the glade, his eye unconsciously picked up a sign in the earth beside a fallen tree trunk. The print had no heel. A moccasin. It was too deep and clear to have been made in dry earth.

How long ago was the last rain? He could remember one two weeks ago. He was safe, then. He rose and swung on down the hill, an aimless, loose-jointed motion entering his body. Within sound of the river below, he came across more sign. It was a broken arrow shaft. It looked like it had been made from a shoot of early berry alder, and had two wavering red lines painted from the feathers down either side. That would be Dakota. A strange apprehension filled him, and he began to look for those prints again. He found them. Suspicion of years formed a premonition in him, and he began following the prints. The sign cut to a ford in the Wind River.

He crossed through the freezing, knee-deep water, cut more sign on the other side, went on in dripping leggings. It was still old sign, and it was what fooled him. He almost stumbled into the man. The first sight of him caused Innes to drop into service berries at the very edge of the glade. The rattle caused the man to turn his head toward him in a swift jerk.

Recognition closed Innes's throat off against breath. It was Wisapa. The Dakota lay in a buffalo robe, propped up against a mossy boulder at the edge of the park. His face was even more haggard than Innes's, great, black hollows beneath the oblique cheek bones, the eyes sunken till they seemed to be staring from the sockets of a skull. There was so little flesh left that Innes could see the formation of the man's teeth through the skin.

The two of them stared at each other for a long time, without speaking. Innes saw the Indian's parfleche bag opened on the ground, its effects scattered over the earth. Beyond that was Innes's old Yerger. The Indian must have taken the rifle from Innes's camp back there in Jackson Hole, when Ryker had first jumped him.

Innes worked back into the thicket. His first impulse was to run. But the puzzle of this held him by a tenuous thread. He made a complete circle of the park. The only other sign he found was of heeled boots and three unshod horses, going out to the east, and they were as old as the sign he had seen before.

Finally he circled back to where he was nearest his rifle, but still in cover. He had moved so silently the Indian had not heard him approach this second time, and sat staring straight ahead. Sniffing the air, cocking his ears, waiting for a painfully long time, Innes at last rose and darted out, scooping up the gun and shot pouch and powder horn from where they lay on the ground, then ran back into timber.

He started to load, when, unaccountably, the thought came into his mind. This was the same gun with which his grand-father had killed George MacAlister back in Virginia. With a strangled sound in his throat, he almost flung the Yerger from him. Would it never stop haunting him? No matter which way he turned? Not just the MacAlisters themselves. Everything he did. Every move he made. It caused him painful effort to retain the piece and load it.

"All right," he said from his covert, "I've got it loaded now. If you don't want a chunk of Galena in you, tell me what this is."

The man stared at him in utter silence. As weak and haggard as he looked, his eyes were filled with bitter, black defiance. Innes kept going over the signs, trying to obliterate his unreasoning suspicion with the logic of it. There just couldn't be anybody else around. With the memory of Brahan, his finger kept twitching against the trigger. It was no more than the Indian deserved. Then a new thought struck him. Wisapa had a bow, and no Indian would waste precious lead on game. Innes reached into his shot pouch. He had carried extra bars of Galena lead in his possible sack, but there had been only fourteen molded balls in his tiger tail pouch. He counted them carefully. There were thirteen in the pouch, and the one in the gun.

"Ryker shot Brahan?" he said.

The man's eyes had been on his hand in that pouch, and the Indian must have realized what he was figuring. But there was no answer.

"You might save your life," said Innes.

Still no answer. Finally Innes squirmed in behind the rock, trying to remain in cover, and caught Wisapa beneath the armpits, dragging him back into the shelter of timber. Here he threw off the buffalo robe. Caked blood covered the man's buckskins. They had been cut away from the hip, and a crude buckskin bandage applied. When Innes lifted this off, the ghastly, swollen infection of the wound sickened him.

A sense of purpose he had not held for months filled his movements now. He went into the clearing, scrambling through the parfleche bag for the flint and steel he hoped was there. He found some, and gathered up dead wood for a fire. There was a brass trade kettle still lashed on an *aparejo* that had been thrown from a horse. Innes pulled the kettle from the pack saddle and filled it with river water. While it was coming to a boil, he hunted for black root along the river bottoms, gathering a double handful. Putting as much as he could in his mouth, he started chewing on it, while he cleansed the wound with the boiled water. Then he rubbed the pulpy poultice of black root into the infection.

He marveled at the Indian's stoicism. The pain would have been unbearable to a white man in that weakened condition.

Bandaging the wound with strips torn from the *aparejo*, Innes dragged Wisapa in close to the fire, getting enough wood to keep it going should he be gone all night. He piled this within reach of the man, and set off for some game.

That was easy for a man with a gun. He found a buffalo wallow torn apart by rutting bulls, and followed fresh sign into a meadow where a great, shaggy beast snorted as it saw him. Innes maneuvered for a heart shot. The detonation of the gun was followed by the beast's roar of agony. The buffalo shook his head, staggered from one side to the other. A great gout of blood spurted from its shaggy coat. It steadied itself, lowering its short-horned head, and rushed for Innes. He turned to leap aside, and the beast plowed blindly by. It ran for a few yards beyond, then halted again, and with a low, rumbling groan fell on its side.

He skinned it, cut steaks and back fat and short ribs, cleaned the intestines and looped them over a stick. All this he put in the bloody hide, gathered up the four leg ends, and carried it back to camp.

When Wisapa saw what Innes had brought, a strange, puzzled light tempered the bitterness of his eyes. Innes cut up the steaks to season a broth he made in the trade kettle. He found pemmican in the parfleche bag and thickened the broth with this. He fed it to Wisapa slowly. Then he toasted the intestines over hot coals till it was crispy brown, and fed it in small pieces to the Indian. This was a delicacy almost as cherished as beaver tail to an Indian. Finally Innes cooked two great steaks for himself, eating the first one almost raw. After the meal, he hunted in the *aparejo* for some fleshing materials to clean the buffalo hide. He found the tools in a little buckskin bag. There was the leg bone of a wolf, serrated on one edge, for scraping the hide. He staked the great, shaggy skin out, and began fleshing.

"Why are you doing that?" asked Wisapa.

His voice was stronger, and Innes gave no sign of his surprise at this abrupt overture. "If we're going to stay here long, we'll need some robes," he said. "Winter isn't too far off, and that ice field across the river don't help any right now. Looks of that wound, I don't think you can travel much for a while."

"Perhaps never," said Wisapa. "I have not been able to move from the hips down since Ryker shot me."

Innes lifted his head to stare at the man, and all the pieces dropped into place. The Indian had lain there, like that, paralyzed, starving, for almost two weeks.

"You didn't shoot Brahan, then?" said Innes hopefully.

"No," said Wisapa. "Ryker came into this country many years ago, trapping and trading with the Indians. It is how I got to know him. I had worked for Hudson's Bay since I was very young. It is how I knew English. Ryker engaged me as an interpreter, and finally as a partner. He convinced me that it would ruin the country for anyone but him to find Lost River. If another trapper discovered it, more of his breed would flood in. The trapper always opens the door for the settler, and with the settler, war. The Indian always loses. But Ryker promised if I helped him find Lost River, he would keep its secret. He also gave me his word there would be no killing over it. After we met the young MacAlister at Bridger's Fort, and found out they possessed the map, Ryker and I camped above Hoback Cañon. He said he would try to make a deal with Roderick, but he kept putting it off. We were on the bluffs when you came down to the mouth with Brahan."

"But how did you know it was Brahan who had the map?" asked Innes. "He just told you at Fort Bridger that if you wanted it, look up the MacAlisters."

"The older brother was in our camp once," said Wisapa. "I think he betrayed Brahan in return for a share of Lost River."

The emotion flooding Innes caused him to tremble, sick at his stomach, and then that resolved itself into a hate for Elgin he knew would never die. He gestured at the Indian's legs, speaking gutturally. "How did this happen?"

"When Ryker killed Brahan, my face was turned from him," said Wisapa. "We quarreled here, and he shot me. He must have thought I was dead. He went through the *aparejos* on my pack animal to get what he needed and scattered the rest on the ground like that, and left me lying in the clearing." He paused, staring at Innes. Finally he spoke again, in a quiet resignation. "Ryker has the map, not I."

"I didn't think you had it," said Innes.

"Then why are you saving my life?" asked the Indian.

"Is it inconceivable to you that I just can't go off and let you die?" asked Innes.

The Dakota stared at him for a long period without answering. "That is a very simple reason," he said at last. "Perhaps that is why it is such a good reason. It is not many white men I have called *kola.*"

"What's that?"

"In my language, it means friend."

A faint, strange warmth pervaded Innes. It was the same feeling he had felt when Brahan called them brother Scots. Then, with a bitter, habituated response, he choked it off.

"Don't make the mistake of doing that," he said. "Anybody who calls me friend is as good as signing his own death warrant."

V

Summer waned. The red haws began turning brown, and the fireweed was losing its flame. Innes built them a dugout against the bluff near the clearing, and for weeks applied the black root to draw the infection from the wound. It was a slow, painful process, with Wisapa delirious and close to death much of the time, but, when the first wedge of geese *honked* south from Bull Lake, the wound had really begun to heal.

The paralysis remained, however, and in mid-September Innes built a travois upon which to lay the Indian and, taking the place of a horse, hauled him the twenty-some miles to Warm Springs Creek. Here, on a rolling sagebrush bench, was a geyser, known to the Indians for its curative qualities. With the wound healed, Innes could bathe the man daily in its warm, bubbling water, and massage his legs for several hours after each bath. The first snow bore down the branches of the spruces beneath the ledge until they looked like great, white umbrellas, but Innes did not let it prevent their bath that day, and a Chinook melted the banks before nightfall.

Wisapa could move his legs by now, and was gaining weight. More snow came, turning the slopes white, and this was how Innes saw the tracks.

He had come from the dugout they had built just under the ledge one morning, looking about for signs of game to replenish their larder. He sighted what he thought were *wapiti* tracks south of them, emerging from snow-blanketed timber, crossing a park, and disappearing again. He told Wisapa he would be back soon, and slipped into the buffalo coat he had made for himself.

The wind was coming from the southwest, and, heading south toward the track, he climbed to the ridge where he could sight the animal. He was close enough to the tracks then to see that they were made by only one pair of feet. He dropped to his hunkers beside some fir, realizing how much his suspicion, his wariness had been dulled by these last weeks with the Indian.

Had the man seen him? How could he help it? The dugout was in plain view from the park those tracks crossed, and he had been standing at the door for a long period. An awesome prescience filled him with a knowledge of whom this was as certainly as if he had seen the man. His belly began to constrict with that cramping pain. He could get out now. He didn't want to face this. He didn't want to kill. There was no sense to it. And he would have to, if he stayed—he knew that. It was stupid. It was animal. There was utterly no reason for it. Yet, if he stayed, it was either kill or be killed.

Then, get out. He glanced down at the dugout. There would be no returning to it. It was too much in view. He would be a perfect target. And Wisapa, after all these patient weeks? The man was still sick, barely able to move. He would be alone. Or would they let him survive? After they found an Innes had befriended him? His head turned from side to side in that painful, frustrated way. His every instinct was to run. He didn't think he had ever wanted to do anything so badly in his life.

The sound of the shot filled the cañon. His horrified eyes stared at the furrow in the snow a foot from his elbow. Then he headed downslope in a desperate, blind run, hunting for better cover. The detonation had shattered against a granite uplift of a high ridge behind this one, sweeping back across the valley to strike the other slope in a hundred echoes, multiplied to a thousand by the crags and rock faces on that side, till the valley seemed filled with roaring, laughing, clapping explosions.

He went belly down behind a granite ledge, hands working with the feverish skill of the countless other times he had loaded that Yerger. He dumped powder down the barrel without bothering to measure it in the charge cup. He had long ago used up his linen patches, and he fumbled a buckskin patch from his shot pouch, greasing it with bear tallow from a trap in the stock of the gun, clapping it onto the ball of Galena lead.

Ramming this into the barrel, patch between the ball and powder, he searched the timber vainly, below and above, for movement that would give the gunman away. He called to the man in a final desperation.

"MacAlister, damn you, don't do this! I don't want to fight you. I didn't kill your son. Do you hear that, Roderick? I didn't kill Brahan. I don't want this. I don't want to shoot you. Don't make me. Please, don't do this . . . !"

He stopped as he sighted movement. It was above him now, in the cedars, stunted and twisted by the wind. Below him was that park, fifty yards of open snowfield in which he would be a perfect target. Yet this rock ledge was not high enough to protect him. He could not run. It was shoot, or nothing.

"MacAlister, please, I'm begging you. Can't you hear me, Roderick? I don't want to fight you. Damn you, I don't want to fight!"

The flash of light on gun metal stopped his shouting and brought habituated reaction. Without conscious volition, he brought up his own gun, and felt the velvety pressure of the trigger. Curly maple jarred his face as the stock bucked into him with the explosion. He was still partly deafened by it when the other man's bullet hit the top of the granite shelf in front of Innes, screaming off in a ricochet. Sharp rock chipped into Innes's face. The cañon was filled with those laughing, clapping echoes again.

Then, from the trees up there, a figure staggered out into the snow. He had no rifle, and he was holding his belly with both hands, doubling over more and more as he stumbled through the deep drift downhill. Finally he was jackknifed so low Innes could see the back of his neck, and the man over on his face.

Innes waited for a long time with reloaded gun, searching the surrounding terrain. Finally he rose and made his way to the man, rolling him over. It wasn't Roderick. It was Elgin.

Innes dropped to his knees beside the man, that awful, bitter despair filling him again. The dark face still mocked him, staring up in sardonic death. Knowing it had been Elgin who betrayed Brahan to Ryker, Innes could feel no sense of vengeance, no vindication. He could feel nothing except the black, sinking, overpowering knowledge that this was only further fulfillment of the curse. Now Roderick would be hunting him on two counts.

"Damn you," he told Elgin between his teeth in a desperate, sobbing way, "damn you."

VI

Wisapa had the wisdom and understanding not to try and penetrate the somber, uncommunicative mood that shrouded Innes. They hardly spoke all day long, and the Scotsman spent most of the day and half the night searching the forest for sign. It had become an obsession with him. More than once he rose up in his robes in the middle of the night and asked Wisapa if that were not Roderick MacAlister standing in the doorway.

He still tended the Indian, however. The bitter chill of full winter gripped the valley now, and the streams were iced over, and game was scarce. The two men were on a diet of jerked meat and pemmican Innes had prepared for this contingency. Then, one day, a band of Shoshones appeared, traveling south. Innes had a good store of buffalo robes, and quill work Wisapa had worked on during his convalescence, and, for this, they traded a couple of mangy ponies. Innes had not meant to use the horses as soon as this. It was the word the Shoshones dropped, just before they left, that gave him the impetus.

They said a giant Scotsman had been sighted in the Wind River. With him was a young woman. They were traveling eastward.

The next day Innes set to work on a buffalo saddle for Wisapa that would carry him comfortably. He finished it that night, and they left the dugout at dawn, with the Indian riding an old beefsteak paint, and their robes and food packed on the weedy mare. The Dakota country was east of the Big Horns, and it was a bitter, grueling journey. They reached Tensleep Creek, named that by the Indians for the number of days it took to reach from Colter's Hell. From the heights above Tensleep Gorge, they could see over onto the eastern slopes, and, although Wisapa allowed no expression to reach his face, there was an excited gleam to his eyes as they ranged over home country. Toward evening, they caught sight of a trapper's cabin snuggled into a cairn halfway down the cliffs into the gorge. There were tracks over the snow, too. Neither of the men cared to stop, however—Innes being driven by his haunting fear of Roderick, Wisapa wanting to reach his people as soon as possible. Innes did not notice when the fairly warm, west wind began to shift, but Wisapa pulled the horse up sharply.

"We had better seek cover, *kola*. That shifting wind brings a blizzard in this area quicker than you would believe. That cabin?"

"There's no point in turning back that far," said Innes.

"More point than you realize," said Wisapa. "You don't know this section as I do. The blizzards are violent and deadly."

Reluctantly Innes wheeled in the other direction. Already the chill of the wind was penetrating his buffalo coat. Soon sleet began to fall, and they were pushed heavily along by the force of the growing storm at their backs. At last visibility was such they did manage to find a trail down. He felt a tug at the lead line in his hand, and whirled to see the mare slipping over. His own shout was muffled as he made a last, vain effort to drag the kicking beast back onto the shelf, and then he had to let go, and the horse toppled off with a wild whinny that had no sound in the blizzard. Sickly Innes turned back to Wisapa, lifting him off the other animal, for fear the same thing might happen to the Indian. He half carried him the rest of the way down.

VII

Reaching the cabin, he tried to open the door, but it would not give. Apparently it was barred from within, and he began to throw the weight of his body against it, feeling the give of rawhide hinges. Then it was thrown open, and he found himself facing a short, massive bear of a man holding an immense Ketland-McCormick in one fist.

"Don't beat the door down," said Ryker. "I wouldn't keep a dog out in a storm like this. Come in, my friends." He chuckled ironically, hoarsely, deep in his throat. "Both my good friends."

Dazed by the storm, Innes could do nothing but stare at the man. Then, answering the imperative wave of Ryker's pistol, he carried Wisapa in. Innes lowered him to a sitting position against the wall. The Indian had not taken his eyes from Ryker, and they had a wide, unblinking glitter to them that started disturbing the man.

"Where's the others?" asked Ryker.

"What others?" said Innes, watching the pistol.

"You know what others," said Ryker, glancing in a quick, nervous way at Wisapa, then edging to the door to look out. "I saw tracks on the other side of the gorge this morning."

"We didn't come in by that side," said Innes. "What are you doing here, anyway? Tensleep can't be Lost River."

"Close to it, if the map's right," said Ryker. He had to lean all his weight against the door to shut it, and stood that way, without having dropped the bar into place, his body trembling to the buffeting wind beating at the portal. "I built this cabin when the snow started. Been using it as a base to hunt Lost River ever since."

"Did it strike you," said Wisapa, "that he can only shoot one of us with that pistol?"

"Now wait a minute!" Ryker turned the gun on Wisapa in automatic reaction, then jerked it back to Innes, as the trapper shifted his weight faintly. "Wait a minute. I let you in, didn't I?"

"And you'll kill us when you're good and ready," said Innes. "You already tried to kill Wisapa once."

Wisapa turned himself about and dragged himself bodily into a standing position against the wall.

Innes saw what he meant to do, and moved around onto the other side of Ryker so they would approach him from two different directions. Ryker looked from the Indian to the trapper, apparently unwilling to believe their intent. Under ordinary circumstances, Innes would have thought it a foolish thing to do. But it was a certainty in his mind that Ryker did not intend to let either of them live. It might as well be this way as any. And knowing the implacability of Wisapa's purpose, it just wasn't in Innes to let him do it alone. Wisapa started dragging himself down the wall, and Innes took a step toward Ryker. That it was still inconceivable to Ryker showed in his twisted face.

"Don't be crazy," he said, trying to laugh, yet brandishing the gun from one to the other. "There's no need for me to kill you. I'll cut you in for shares. We'll find it together, and I'll cut you in for shares."

"Like you did Brahan?" said Innes.

The sudden, full shock of realizing they meant to go through with it stamped a bestial contortion on Ryker's face. He twisted from side to side, turning the gun on Wisapa, cocking the flat, goose-necked hammer with a desperate hook of his thumb, sweeping the big, brass-bound weapon back toward Innes.

"No, listen. Don't be crazy. This is crazy, Innes. I'll kill you. . . ."

"Only one of us, Ryker."

"And it'll be you, Innes."

"Will it, Ryker?" said Wisapa.

Ryker whirled toward him. His eyes widened, glittered. The

gun jerked higher. Only one more step.

The door shuddered suddenly beneath a heavy, buffeting weight, knocking Ryker forward so hard his gun went off at the floor. Innes jumped at him, grabbing the gun arm. Ryker twisted beneath him, rolled to the floor, wrenching the gun arm loose to beat at him with the heavy weapon. Wisapa threw his body across the arm, pinning it to the floor.

Screaming curses, Ryker doubled up his legs to kick out from beneath Innes. A foot caught Innes in the belly, and he slammed against the wall. Wisapa tried to stop Ryker from rolling over on him, but the bearded man possessed immense strength. He left that one arm beneath Wisapa and reached around in a bear hug with the other, putting his weight atop the Indian. Then he caught the roached hair and beat the Dakota's head into the puncheon floor.

Gasping in pain, Innes threw himself back at Ryker, clawing him off Wisapa. For that one instant, he was on the man's back. He thrust a knee into the small of it, hooked desperate arms around Ryker's neck, heaved upward.

Ryker's body bent like a bow in the leverage. There was a loud, snapping sound, like a breaking branch. Ryker's body formed no more pressure for the grip; it was like bending a limp sack. Innes released him, letting the lolling head drop to the floor. The mouth gaped; the eyes were open, glassy. The man was dead.

Innes was trembling heavily. He realized it must be reaction. At the time, moving in on Ryker with the gun, he had felt no particular emotion. But it must have created a terrible tension, for he felt so weak and shaken now he could hardly focus his gaze. Then he saw what had come against the door. It was open now, with the howling blizzard piling snow and sleet a foot high across the threshold. The girl crouched there, staring in horror at them through eyes streaming tears from the wind. The name left Innes in whispered shock.

"Nairn."

"Innes," she said gutturally.

"Those were your tracks Ryker saw across the gorge."

"We were following you," she panted. "We've been following you for months. Dad tried to leave me at several posts, but I came after him every time. I didn't realize we were this close behind. We found that dugout on Wind River and figured it was yours. And the grave. . . ."

"You know who it was?" he asked. They were crouched there, staring at each other in some sort of dazed spell, oblivious to the shouting gale, unwilling to move.

"Elgin," she said in a small voice.

"I had to kill him, Nairn," he almost sobbed.

She stared at him a long moment, an indefinable expression twisting her face. Then it smoothed out, and she was looking at him in that wide-eyed way.

"I still love you, Innes."

"You can't!" His shout was animal, guttural. "I killed your brother. Don't you hear? You can't love me."

"I do, I do!" The spell was broken now, and they were both stumbling to their feet. She caught at him. "I do love you, Innes, and you've got to get out of here. Father's behind me somewhere. He'll be coming in. We were about a mile beyond the cabin when the blizzard started. I lost him on the way back. You've got to leave. He's not the same, Innes. He was bad enough to begin with. He would have killed you at the first if I hadn't stopped him. But now he's crazy. He's possessed with it, Innes. He thinks you killed his two sons, and he's possessed with it."

"No!" His shout was sharp-edged, and he released her, backing up against the wall. There was a strange determination in his face. "You asked me once to stop running, Nairn. It's no use. It follows me wherever I go. Ryker wasn't just a man, killing and stealing and hunting for a fortune in furs. He was part of the curse. It touches everybody who comes near me. I can't escape it by running."

"Please, Innes, Father'll kill you."

"Let him. What's the difference? I don't care any more. I'm through running. You're the only thing I ever really wanted, anyway, and I can't have you, so what's the difference? Do you hear that, Roderick? Come on, kill me. I don't care."

"Innes! You're getting as crazy as Father. Don't. Please. Get out. Please."

"No!" His wild shout lifted above the storm, and he raised his head to roar into it. "Do you hear that, Roderick? I'm through running."

"Aye, Innes, I hear it," said Roderick MacAlister, appearing out of the storm like a ponderous giant. He swayed there a moment in the doorway, staring ghoulishly at Innes. He was muffled to the chin in a plaid Mackinaw. Ice had formed on his brows, giving them a hoary, frosted look. His eyes were red-rimmed and gleaming with a feverish, fanatical light. Innes had seen the same look in Cheyenne Sun Dancers at the peak of their crazed orgies, when the terrible tortures of the ceremonies had robbed them of all reason.

Roderick reached back for the hilt of his claymore where he had slung it in a case behind his back.

"Father!" screamed Nairn, throwing herself on him. "Roderick!"

"Out of me way, ye ree loun. I'm goin' to kill this Lalland, Innes," said Roderick. With one arm he swept her aside, yanking the huge sword from its scabbard and swinging it down before him. Innes stood back against the wall. He could feel fear in himself. He wouldn't deny that. Yet his bitter resolve to stop running from something that had haunted him all his life kept his body spread-eagled against the logs.

"Brahan, Innes," said Roderick, moving toward him. "Elgin. That was Elgin, wasn't it? That grave back on the Wind River. He was trailing you. He left even before I did. My sons, Innes, both my sons." He stopped a couple of paces away from Innes, breathing heavily, a sly, waiting, expectant look on his face. As Innes made no move, surprise showed in those little, red-rimmed eyes for a moment. Then he drew in a great, gasping breath, and let the shout go. "Thig Ris, Innes, Thig Ris!"

The sword made a dull glitter in the dusky light. Innes could not inhibit his responses. They jerked him aside uncontrollably in the last instant. The blade struck the log wall with a clanging shudder.

"Thig Ris," bellowed MacAlister, "at it again!" He heaved up with his prodigious blade. Innes did not see how Nairn came in. She caught her father's arm, screaming at him.

"Let go, ye whingin' wean, let go. I'm killin' an Innes."

It was with his sword arm he swept her back. Perhaps it was the pain in her cry that penetrated his fogged mind. Or the horror filling Innes's eyes, staring at Nairn, as she staggered back with the blood spurting from the wound that blade had made in her side. She struck the wall and collapsed in a heap. Roderick dropped his sword and staggered over to her, falling to his knees. He cradled her limp body in one arm, pawing at the blood covering her dress. At first, calling her name, his voice was a sobbing contrition. It began to grow louder as she did not answer. He felt for her heart.

"Nairn!" he screamed finally. "Nairn, answer me, say I haven't killed ye! Yure own father, Nairn . . . he couldn't kill ye . . . tell me I haven't!" He let her sink back, his hand slipping away from her heart, a brassy film covering his eyes. Then, with a great, maniacal scream, he heaved to his feet. "Nairn," he howled like a bereft beast, "Nairn, Nairn, Nairn!" His voice was lost in the storm as he lunged out the door, screaming it over and over.

"Roderick!" shouted Innes. "Don't! You'll go off the cliff . . . !"

It was impulse more than anything else driving him out after the man. It couldn't have been thought. The last few moments seemed to have shocked all capacity for that from him. He stumbled out into the blizzard, catching sight of the gigantic, plunging figure ahead of him. Roderick seemed to halt for a moment on the edge of the cliff. Innes shouted at him again. Then his figure was gone.

Innes staggered to the bluff, staring downward. He wondered, dully, whether the man had fallen, or had deliberately cast himself off. He sank to his knees, eyes still turned down into the gorge.

Murk hid the bottom, hundreds of feet below. It seemed to draw him, pull at him. *Why not?* There was nothing left for him. He knew now for a certainty that Roderick had thrown himself off deliberately. And he could understand why. It was the logical thing when there was nothing left in life. It would be so easy. He squinted his eyes shut against the sight of Nairn's dead body back there in the cabin, of Elgin's dead body, of the pain in Brahan's dead face, of John Donn lying there in a Shoshone grave, of the chain of tragedy and death that he had left on his back trail.

And now it was over. He would finish it. He could face no more of it. Slowly, inexorably the defeat inclined his body forward.

"Kola!"

Innes jerked, straightened, seemed to lift from a trance. When he wheeled about, he saw Wisapa, dragging himself down across the trail. Innes turned reluctantly back to the man, shaking his head.

"The woman is not dead," Wisapa told him. "I stanched the blood. It's a bad wound, but, if we can get her to my people, I think she will live. You saved my life, *kola*. You can save hers."

Innes's heart leaped against his ribs with painful force. He ran past the Indian, into the room where Nairn lay on the floor, covered by a robe. He dropped to his knees beside her, catching a pale hand in his. She looked up weakly.

"Something must have snapped in your father when he thought he had killed you," said Innes, answering the question in her eyes. "He ran out. The cliffs. . . ."

She closed her eyes, a poignant grief pinching her face, whitening it. Her breast lifted beneath the robe with the breath she took. Finally she spoke carefully.

"You're not to blame, Innes. He brought it on himself. As much as he meant to me, it's the truth."

"You'll be all right," he said. "We'll get you to Wisapa's people."

"Of course I will. You'll stay with me, won't you, Innes? It's over now. You've beaten the curse." She must have seen the way he squinted his eyes and shook his head from side to side, for she lurched up, catching feebly at his arm. "Yes, you have. You stood up to it. You stopped running. You refused to perpetuate it. And you won. There's no reason for it to go on. We're together, aren't we? An Innes and a MacAlister. That in itself refutes the whole thing."

"She's right," said Wisapa. He held up the map and journal of Father Escobar that he must have found on Ryker. "You have these now. We can find Lost River. With you, I know it will not harm my people."

Innes took the book and map. Ryker must have been building a fire in the fireplace when they entered, for the coals were still glowing. Innes put some more wood on, and, when the flames began to leap, he threw the map and book on it.

"That way you can be sure your people won't suffer," he told Wisapa. "We couldn't really wipe the slate clean with those around. It's what started all this trouble."

Wisapa bowed his head humbly. "You are a greater man than I thought, *kola*. When I tell my people what you did, you will have their lifelong respect. It is something few white men can command."

That vagrant smile caught at Innes's lips, flashing across them like sunlight on dark waters for a moment. He moved back to Nairn, taking her hand. Then he looked into the flames, licking about the little, leather-covered book, and for a moment the mysticism of his Celtic blood asserted itself, and he spoke to the fire with all the naïve sincerity of a savage propitiating some ancient god.

"Do you see this, Alister Mor?" he said softly. "An Innes and a MacAlister joined. That's something you never believed would happen, isn't it? I think that's something all your curses in the world can't harm."

"I *know* that's something they can't harm," said Nairn.

ABOUT THE AUTHOR

Les Savage, Jr. was born in Alhambra, California and grew up in Los Angeles. His first published story was "Bullets and Bull-whips," accepted by the prestigious magazine, Street & Smith's *Western Story*. Almost ninety more magazine stories followed, all set on the American frontier, many of them published in Fiction House magazines such as *Frontier Stories* and *Lariat Story Magazine* where Savage became a superstar with his name on many covers. His first novel, *Treasure of the Brasada*, appeared from Simon & Schuster in 1947. Due to his preference for historical accuracy, Savage often ran into problems with book editors in the 1950s who were concerned about marriages between his protagonists and women of different races—a commonplace on the real frontier but not in much Western fiction in that decade. Savage died young, at thirty-five, from complications arising out of hereditary diabetes and elevated cholesterol. However, as a result of the censorship imposed on many of his works, only now are they being fully restored by returning to the author's original manuscripts. Among Savage's finest Western stories are *Fire Dance at Spider Rock* (Five Star Westerns, 1995), *Medicine Wheel* (Five Star Westerns, 1996), *Coffin Gap* (Five Star Westerns, 1997), *Phantoms in the Night* (Five Star Westerns, 1998), *The Bloody Quarter* (Five Star Westerns, 1999), *In The Land of Little Sticks* (Five Star Westerns, 2000), *The Cavan Breed* (Five Star Westerns, 2001), and *Danger Rides the River* (Five Star Westerns, 2002). Much as Stephen

Crane before him, while he wrote, the shadow of his imminent death grew longer and longer across his young life, and he knew that, if he was going to do it at all, he would have to do it quickly. He did it well, and, now that his novels and stories are being restored to what he had intended them to be, his achievement irradiated by his powerful and profoundly sensitive imagination will be with us always, as he had wanted it to be, as he had so rushed against time and mortality that it might be. *Arizona Showdown* will be his next Five Star Western.